Anonymous

On a Western Campus

Stories and sketches of undergraduate life

Anonymous

On a Western Campus
Stories and sketches of undergraduate life

ISBN/EAN: 9783337423919

Printed in Europe, USA, Canada, Australia, Japan

Cover: Foto ©Andreas Hilbeck / pixelio.de

More available books at **www.hansebooks.com**

On A Western Campus.

STORIES AND SKETCHES OF
UNDERGRADUATE LIFE

By

THE CLASS OF
NINETY-EIGHT.

IOWA COLLEGE,
GRINNELL, IOWA.

Illustrated by
FRANK WING.

Buffalo, New York:
CHARLES WELLS MOULTON.
1897.

CONTENTS.

—

I. Co-Education.

II. Portraits.

III. Recreation.

IV. In Serious Vein.

LIST OF ILLUSTRATIONS.

Prefatory Note.

THE immediate function of this little volume is to serve as the annual production of the Junior class in Iowa College. It is believed, however, that a somewhat radical and significant departure has been made from the typical "Junior annual" idea, with a result which deserves attention beyond the limits of local college interests.

These stories and sketches have been written with the view of presenting, mainly in the spirit of realistic interpretation and principally as they are observed to-day, varied scenes in the "human comedy" of a co-educational college between the Missouri and the Mississippi. Not so much attempt has been made to reproduce the specific shades of "local color," as to paint such characteristics as are essentially representative of numerous institutions of similar type in the West.

Some study is given to the conditions of the

school in its early days—the days of "the War"; and some report is made of the capricious hostility of Nature, never more emphatic than in the historic calamity of this prairie college. The repose of puritanic ideas, transplanted directly from New England, is seen mildly disturbed by the influences of modern scientific education; the intensity of athletic strife is felt, and the exultant thrill of hardly-won victory; even the pranks of students upon faculty—so much more terrible in this "wild and wooly West" than in the Great Eastern Universities!—have not escaped the recording pen.

While the writers have endeavored to give a definite artistic unity to the volume, it can not be expected that every piece will satisfy the fastidious, in style, construction or subject. Perfection in short-story writing is a more difficult attainment, according to the initiated, than ordinary success in the novel. The undergraduate has no opportunity for the ten years' apprenticeship of Maupassant or Bourget; and he has stronger temptation to deny free, original expression to his individuality, than one of his own age unrestrained by the conventions of college life.

Nevertheless, it is hoped that this little collection of stories may arouse attention, approval and even somewhat of serious criticism, especially among progressive teachers of literature and their students. To such hands the writers are willing to entrust their fortunes, believing that interest in the processes of art, as of life, is no less noble than the delight in ripened fruits, and remembering the spirit of the poet who wrote:

"They are perfect—how else? They shall never change:
We are faulty—why not? We have time in store."

GRINNELL, Iowa, May the First, 1897.

I.

CO-EDUCATION.

a whole gymnasium in itself for Milburn."

Two Students of Science.

"THERE! I think I'll have as good a yield of iodoform as anybody. I guess I'll rest my nerves a little while that stuff settles;" and casting his big apron aside he proceeded to climb, hand over hand, up a vertical iron water-pipe which ran through the hall just outside the laboratory door. The pipe was held secure in its place by a joint which came in contact with a beam overhead, and was known by the chemistry students as the "greased pole," since it was a whole gymnasium in itself for Milburn, who was now taking exercise on it.

Soon he appeared again in the door and called, "Say Sister! come on and climb the 'greased pole' once, it will do you good." Miss Keller had received a similar invitation several times before, and while she showed no particular signs of responding to it, she resolved to practice the exercise in the Gymna-

(17)

sium, and surprise Milburn by performing sometime when she was dressed in her tennis suit.
"I can't do it now," she replied. "Some
time when I have my bloomers on I'll try it."

"Now is the accepted time," said Hicks, a
young man working at qualitative analysis at
the end of the room, and he began to whistle,
"Why do you wait, dear brother?"

Miss Keller was the only girl in Hawkeye
College who was taking advanced work in
chemistry, and the others working in the laboratory with her insisted that she ought to
have been a boy. It was a favorite trick of
Milburn's to make a profound bow in her
direction when he came in to work after dinner, and say, "Good afternoon, gentlemen!"
It was now nearly three years since they began
work together in the laboratory, but he
had not yet become entirely accustomed to
the idea of a girl taking a science for a major;
or, what is more probable, he chose to make it
appear that the idea was novel to him, and
though he usually addressed her as "Sister,"
he enjoyed referring to her as one of the boys.
When he had been in the beginning class with

her and she had told him that her majors were chemistry and biology he had quite surprised her by saying, "A scientific *girl!* *My gracious!* I didn't know the Lord ever made any."

When she found out that he was interested in social science, and lived at the college settlement, and sometimes preached in neighboring school-houses and adjacent villages, she returned his surprise by saying: "*My gracious!* *A scientific preacher!* I didn't know the Lord ever made any."

They evidently regarded each other as curious freaks, and from that moment there began to spring up between them a strong brotherly and sisterly feeling.

He now came hurriedly back to his desk and began to put it in order. It was nearly four o'clock and he wanted to play tennis.

"See here," said he turning to Miss Keller, "if you had been industrious, you might have been through now, and had time to play tennis with people who *work.*" He said this with an air of sternness wholly assumed and ran down into the basement to put on his sweater.

He soon reappeared bringing a roll of white cloth, suggestive of a white shirt, which he thrust into a drawer under his table.

A young man appeared in the door, apparently waiting for Milburn to come out and play with him. He seemed curious to know what Miss Keller was doing with the two glass tubes, which had metric scales engraved on their sides. They were held by clamps in a vertical position and filled with some colorless liquids. Standing beneath their lower ends, on the white tiling of the table, was a flask filled with another liquid. Miss Keller would turn the stopcock on one of the tubes and let a few drops into the flask below, the contents of which would change from colorless to red; then letting a drop or two fall from the other it would lose its red color. Finally dropping first from the one and then the other, a single drop tinged the liquid with a faint suggestion of crimson and she stopped. Taking a little magnifying glass from the table she read the fine graduations on the sides of the tubes, and found how much of the liquid she had used.

The young man looked inquiringly, and Milburn explained, assuming the most professorial of airs as he did so: "You see she is trying to find exactly how much acid there is in the liquid she has in that flask. So she puts four or five drops of some stuff into it which makes it turn one color when acid and another when alkaline. Now she fills one of those tubes which are called burettes, with a standard alkaline solution and the other with a standard acid solution, each of which contain a known amount of acid or alkali to the cubic centimeter."

"Young man, on the back seat there, you may either pay attention to this recitation or make yourself scarce! Now to continue—she lets the alkali mixture in until the liquid changes color. Then she lets a little of the acid in to equalize the excessive alkali, and finally she gets it neutral. Then she reads this scale and finds how much of alkali she has used in excess of acid. She knows how much acid each fraction of alkali will neutralize, and from this, figures up the amount of acid present in the whole mixture. Is that perfectly plain to you, Lambert? Very well.

Any questions? The class is excused." The two young men were soon out on the campus playing tennis.

"A queer fellow—that Milburn —," said Hicks, "I used to know him in Kansas City. He is as full of fun as the old Nick himself, but he is really a good scientist and a thoroughly careful fellow to have around the laboratory."

"Well I'd like to know," said Smith, a young man watching for the contents of a crucible to fuse, "if a fellow oughtn't to be chuck full of fun crammed down and running over, if he expects to have enough left in him to get a test for after taking such a study as this. Hang this old crucible of stuff! It's been trying this whole hour to fuse and hasn't succeeded yet." And turning quickly he added, "I beg your pardon, Miss Keller, but I really had to swear or do something."

Without looking up from her flask she replied, "O you shall be pardoned, certainly, so long as you confine yourself to such mild profanity under such aggravating circumstances. You are really improving."

Smith began to talk again: "That man Milburn is good too, mighty good for a chemist. A man is always bad and impious if he studies chemistry, especially if that man happens to be a woman." (The girl gave him a withering glance.) "But Milburn isn't a girl so it isn't so surprising that he amounts to something. He spends oceans of time in that college settlement."

"Some say," said Hicks, "that he does it to continue his biological studies and that he is taking the human worm as his specimen."

Miss Keller looked up quickly. "Yes, some may say it," said she, "but I don't believe that it is his principal motive now, though it may have been in the first place. I think it would be a worthy enough one if it were."

"You think it is all right, do you," said Hicks, "to study people over with no other motive than that? I don't believe I'd enjoy being a specimen for your college-house freaks."

The girl smiled and looked up. "All classes of people are the subjects of study for the social scientists, your own class included," said she. "People cannot be helped or help each other to higher planes of existence unless the facts regarding present conditions are known."

"Well, I suppose," said Hicks, "that some facts are necessary, but it looks like a cold-blooded way of going after them, if that is his only motive. I didn't expect you were going to be so eloquent on the subject of sociology."

"I didn't say it was his only motive," she replied, "but if facts are useful, then the finding of them by honest scientific methods is a worthy occupation. He is really trying to help the people around him while he is gaining knowledge from studying them."

"That's right! Stick up for him," said Hicks.

"You ought to see him at the settlement Sunday-school," said she. "He teaches a class and does it sensibly, too. I attended one Sunday when a young man asked him if he believed Aaron's rod really changed into a snake and then back again, and he replied without pause, that he did not."

"What in the name of Jericho did he say to

him?" asked Hicks. "Tell him that the
Bible is a fraud and that he had better follow
the Koran?"

"Hardly. He told them that this story was
really only a poetic way of expressing the influence that a good man like Aaron had over
ignorant and evil-minded people; and that it
was included in the collection of the sacred
writings of the Jews, which we call the Old
Testament. Then he told them something
about the way in which the Bible was com-
piled. Now that's what I call scientific.
The scientific spirit is pervading everything
and we are beginning to study literature, last
of all, scientifically."

"Great Scott!" said Hicks, "what a beast
you're making of science. You're letting it
eat up the universe. I guess I'll prepare myself to be swallowed."

"Never you worry," said she, "the carni-
vora don't eat raw cabbage." Hicks took the
laugh that followed with good grace, and appeared to be squelched. Miss Keller continued: "Milburn is going at religion scientifically." Hicks interrupted again.

"Good gracious! Religion is going to be swallowed too. That carniverous beast will have to have as many stomachs as a cow. He'd have an awful fit of indigestion if he got Miss Keller and religion in the same stomach." The remark was greeted with groans but he did not mind it. He was used to it.

"There are some people," said Miss Keller, who believe Mr. Milburn is dangerous, but he is doing good. Some of the rest of us unorthodox people might well follow his example."

"Well, by all the symbols in the chemical dictionary! or anything else you cold-blooded investigators hold to be sacred and inviolate, I declare that old Milburn has a firm friend in Miss Keller," exclaimed Hicks. "As for me, I've got enough of this scientific business and if I don't flunk at the end of the semester I'll quit you people. Three semesters are enough for me—plenty! I don't see how in the world you third year people managed to survive at all. My health is failing awfully fast and my youth is fading as a flower."

"Sunflower," suggested Smith.

Hicks walked up to the board where the Professor posted special directions. He took one look and then began to rub his eyes. "Well by all the oxides of lead and manganese! Look here, Sister Keller, you had better read this before you stick up for him again. It's very pretty in you, but look at the base ingratitude of the fellow. This is his doing sure." A small group gathered around the place and read the following equation in Milburn's well-known handwriting:

"Keller + Smith + (Hicks)^2 = 1-2 man."

.   .   .   .   .   .

At half past five Miss Keller and Hicks were the only ones remaining in the laboratory. Milburn came rushing through the room and dashed down into the basement to change his clothes for supper, evidently forgetting in his haste, that his coat hung in the laboratory above, and that his shirt was in a drawer under his table. After a time his voice was heard calling, "Hicks! O, Hicks! Come to the head of the stairs a minute."

Hicks obeyed, taking his time about it.

"Say Hicks, please bring my shirt down here, will you? It's in the lower east drawer below my table."

"Well you lazy pup," said Hicks, "I can't see why you don't wait on yourself. Don't you know that my time is valuable? If you call me out here and make me this much trouble again it will go bad with you."

"Why you blooming idiot! don't you see that I've got my sweater off and it's so wet that I can't get it on again, or at least I won't just after taking a bath?"

"You won't, eh, well perhaps you won't."

"You're going to get my shirt for me now aren't you, old boy? That's a nice old fellow!"

"No, I can't say I have any such charitable intentions. I'll have to go back into the lab, and think it over anyway." And he went back.

"O Miss Keller! Sister!" shouted Milburn. "How long before you're going home?"

"About half an hour," she called back.

"Well, but somebody will be eating up my sauce at the club."

"I don't see what I've got to do with your being late to your supper or with your sauce."

"You don't, eh? I wish you'd go home."

"I don't see why."

"I want to come up there after something."

"I have no intention of making a meal of you."

"You'd find him good and tough if you did," said Hicks.

"Say, sister, you go home!"

"I won't do it."

"Say, do you remember that date you have with me for the ball game to-morrow?"

"Yes."

"Well, I'll break it if you don't go home."

"*O Milburn, don't!*"

"I will though; I can't possibly go, if you keep me down here all night."

"I'm not keeping you down there."

"You aren't, eh? Why, good gracious, young lady, if you must know it, there's a part of my raiment in the lab that I must have before I'm presentable in your august presence."

"O, that's it. That's a good one on you.

I think you have no one to blame but yourself. It will give you a chance to reflect on your numerous sins.''

''How can a fellow reflect on his sins when he is mortally sure that some one is eating up his sauce? O my sauce! My sauce!''

''It will give you a perfectly splendid chance to learn to be calm under misfortune.''

''You folks seem to bear up wonderfully under *my* misfortune. Say! I've found the nitro-glycerine C. P. bottle down here, and I'm going to set it off if you don't go into the balance room and shut the door a minute.''

''That's all right,'' shouted Hicks. '' We're above the blamed thing and it will send us right up to glory, but may the Lord have mercy on *your* soul. Your shirt is up here and that will probably go along with us.''

''Say, sister, you go into the balance room a minute and shut the door.''

''Can't afford the time.''

''Yes, you *are awfully* pressed for time. I've a notion to come up there just as I am.''

''Come on,'' shouted Hicks, ''put rings in

your ears and a coat of paint on your body and pass yourself off for a Musquakee Indian."

"Say, sister, I'm coming up there and you'd better leave. I can just *see* that old 'Bones' eating my sauce now. He always does if I am late. Whoopy! Here I come!" Two noisy feet were heard coming up the stairs at a lively rate. Miss Keller, womanlike, sacrificing science to propriety, fled to the balance room and Milburn, triumphant, skipped back bearing his indispensable apparel with him.

Miss Aylesworth's Friend.

ON SCHEDULED time the train came rushing in as if impelled by the eagerness of the new students to reach this Elysium of their dreams. The bell rang out clear and loud. It seemed vieing with the hearty yells which arose from the throng assembled on the platform. They were nearly all students who had come back a day early to visit with old chums and to give the new arrivals a cordial welcome.

When the train stopped a few boys and girls wearing badges, which at once identified them as the new student committee, pressed forward to greet the strangers. As one after another appeared, he was instantly relieved of his luggage with such sincere welcome that he began unconsciously to imbibe the college spirit. Now came a girl more attractive than the rest. She was tall and graceful. Her fall traveling suit became her well. She had a vivacious and dignified manner that was truly fascinating. She attracted the attention of a group of boys standing a little aside and surveying each new comer critically.

"There's an all-right girl. I say, fellows, guess I'll try my luck. Glad I swiped this committee badge now. I thought I might need it," and leaving the group, Leland Curtis was at her side in a moment. His badge served as an introduction and without further ceremony, lifting his hat, he asked to carry her grip.

"My name is Leland Curtis."

"And mine, Frances Wallace," she answered brightly.

"Now if you will give me your checks, I'll see to your baggage. You wish it sent to— ?"

"Mears Cottage, please. You are very kind."

He was off and back in a twinkling, giving the boys a triumphant wink in passing. As they started off down the street, the boys cast envious glances after them.

"Why didn't I have the nerve to do that?" said one regretfully.

"He has a good eye, Curtis has. I'll wager

MISS AYLESWORTH'S FRIEND.   35

my hat against a piece of chalk that they'll
head the list of solid couples this year," said
a second, with the air of one who knew all
the mysteries of a solid couple arrangement.

"Gertrude Manning is in her element now,"
remarked another admiringly.

They looked back toward the train. A
severely plain, modest looking girl had just
appeared. She was not in the least attractive
at first glance. Then one noticed a sensitive,
almost childish expression that was truly ap-
pealing. She seemed timid and the sea of
strange faces bewildered her. It was then
that Gertrude Manning left the merry circle
of friends and came eagerly forward.

"How do you do? You have come to be
one of us I know," she said in her own charming way. "Let me help you with your
bundles." A very grateful look lighted up
the face of the new girl as Miss Manning took
everything into her own hands.

"Now Miss Hampton, I think we are ready
to go. It's just a pleasant walk to your new
home. Let's see, you said your home is in
Auburn, didn't you? I wonder if you hap-

pen to know Miss Aylesworth there? I met her at Lake Geneva last summer."

"Miss Aylesworth! Oh, do you know her? She persuaded me to come here." And Emma Hampton felt her loneliness depart at once; she had found some one who knew some one she knew.

"You see," she went on, "she wanted me to come and my folks couldn't afford to send me. I always liked music and she thought I had such a good voice that she wanted me to have it trained. So she wrote down here and found this place for me at Mrs. Shakelford's. I can help with the housework and the children for my room and board, and my folks can do the rest. It was all her plan."

"That's splendid. I'm glad you have come and I hope you'll soon feel at home among us." When they reached the house she was already in love with the college and wondered if every one were like Miss Manning.

In the meantime, Leland Curtis was walking slowly with Miss Wallace toward Mears Cottage. They reached there all too soon, so he thought, in spite of the fact that he had taken her the longest possible way around, and he was forced to give her up to the tender mercies of Miss Dorcas, the matron of the Cottage. He was exceedingly suspicious of that lady's mercies. He knew her of old. When he was a sporty Freshman he had been devoted to a gay little miss who lived there, and he had always felt responsible for a good share of Miss Dorcas' gray hair and numerous wrinkles.

That night on senior floor some of the girls congregated to talk over the possibilities of the new girls. "Oh! have you met Miss Wallace?"

"Yes, isn't she swell?"

"Isn't she dear!"

"She's simply fine."

"We may count on her for basket-ball. She's played a good deal, she says."

"We must rush her for society too," said a literary enthusiast, the President of Calocagathia.

"Did you see who brought her up to-night?"

"Who?" sounded a chorus of curious voices.

"Leland Curtis."

"He did. Well that's lucky. I'm glad he happened to get her. It will give her a good impression of our youths."

"That's right. Mr. Curtis is the best all-around boy in college."

"Listen! What's that?" and the chatter ceased in an instant.

"Lady Dorcas started on her nightly pilgrimage," said one whose ears were trained to listen for those warning sounds.

"Well, let's adjourn. All in favor please signify by leaving;" and a half dozen girls stole quietly down the hall to their rooms and retired silently by moonlight.

The next day brought the inevitable registering, the arranging of schedules, conflicts to be straightened out, books to be bought, trunks to be unpacked, rooms to be settled; an endless list to the poor Freshmen. But the college machinery was soon in order and all thought was turned to Friday night. Then came the grand reception, when everyone meets everyone else—and in the morning knows no one.

Miss Wallace was the belle of the evening.

She was beautifully gowned and most becomingly, the rich, heavy silk setting off her fine figure well. Her fluffy, golden-brown hair waved back from her forehead bewitchingly, and her dancing brown eyes were irresistible. All the boys were devoted, and the girls, envious. Mr. Curtis thought he had an especial claim to her attention and she seemed to find the claim not irksome.

Miss Manning was there, looking as sweet and charming as ever. She was piloting Emma Hampton through the company, introducing her to old and new students, and making her forget that her skirt was not the latest cut and that her waist was made from an old one of her mother's.

"Mr. Curtis, have you met Miss Hampton?" she said, as Leland came to speak to her.

"I believe not. I'm glad to meet you, Miss Hampton. Hampton," he repeated thoughtfully. "Oh! are you from Auburn? A friend wrote me of a Miss Hampton who was coming from there."

"Yes," and she hesitated a moment, look-

ing at him closely. Then with a look of eager
interest, "Is your friend Miss Aylesworth?
Why of course, and you are that Mr. Curtis."

"Why *that* Mr. Curtis?" he asked laughing.

"Why the Mr. Curtis I've heard so much
about. I have learned to know Miss Aylesworth well and she's done so much for me."

Curtis' smile was credulous and happy.
"She wrote me that you sing a good deal. Is
your work all in the Conservatory?"

"No, I have some college work too. I
can't sing much, but I like to."

Miss Manning just then turned to her
charge to introduce another friend. So the
evening wore away. Emma was happy to have
met Mr. Curtis so soon, and although she was
very critical, for in her eyes no one could be
too good for Alice Aylesworth, she really quite
approved of him.

The next day every one spoke to every one
he cared to, taking it for granted they had met
at the reception. Then work began in earnest and all were busy.

Things ran smoothly and uneventfully during the fall term, the monotony only relieved by a foot-ball game now and then, a class party, a lecture or concert in the Y. M. C. A. course. The fall days were perfect. The air was fresh and invigorating. But the evenings, the moonlight evenings, were simply irresistible to all except the "grinds." It was considered an act of total depravity to study before eight o'clock at least, and all sorts of schemes were concocted for prolonging recreation hours. And so the solid couples began to develop, some slowly, some more rapidly, and were watched very eagerly One especially seemed to interest everybody, probably because of the prominence of the two parties, Frances Wallace and Leland Curtis.

Emma Hampton was the keenest observer of all, but no one knew it. People wondered why Curtis took so much notice of that plain little girl. For Alice's sake he had taken especial care to be kind to her. Then she was a droll little piece, interesting in her way, and he did not mind giving up an evening to her now and then. She did have a sweet voice and he liked to hear her sing. She felt

grateful to him. She liked him. He was as
gallant to her as he was to Miss Wallace. But
above all, because Alice cared for him, he interested her especially. But she did not like
his marked attention to Miss Wallace. It was
beginning to irritate her to see them together.
When she shyly intimated as much, Curtis
would say, in defense of himself, "You see,
Miss Wallace is an awfully nice girl. She's
lots of fun to go with and Alice doesn't mind.
You know it's my last year and I want to
make the most of it."

Miss Wallace confessed to herself that Leland Curtis was a mighty fine fellow. He was
really the only boy in college whose attentions
she cared to accept. But she did not care for
him. She thought too much of some one else,
as semi-weekly letters, written and received,
showed. However, it takes but little to
weave a romance about two names in a college town and soon people declared that they
must be engaged. "Why if they're not, they
ought to be," said one jealous little minx,
who had tried herself to fascinate that popu-
lar fellow and had found him incorrigible.

"They walk together, they ride together, on moonlight nights they go strolling, on stormy nights they sit in the parlor and talk. I'm sure I can't imagine what they find to talk about all the time. Then he takes her to all the receptions and concerts. I'd like to know what more is needed to make them engaged. I wouldn't go with one boy so much, not even with Leland Curtis. I think it's horrid."

"Sour grapes," retorted her room-mate. She was just beginning to know the bliss of having a youth always on hand, of being sure of an invitation to everything; not obliged to wait in awful suspense till the last minute and then buy her own ticket and go with a crowd of girls.

"Why will Leland be so devoted to that Miss Wallace? I don't think he should go with girls at all since Alice isn't here," mused Emma Hampton. "I can't bear to see him with any girl now. Of course it's different for him to come to see me, because I know all about it, and it's only for her sake that he comes, or that I care to have him come. If she were only here, everything would be all right."

But as the year wore away, Emma felt a growing uneasiness. She could not tell what it was exactly. It seemed to have developed unconsciously. Was it that college life had shown her so much of which it seemed she could never be a part? Was it because she had seen such a contrast between herself and other girls? No. She had been happy in her college life and college work. She had found some very dear friends among the girls. Gertrude Manning had proved a friend indeed. Her cordial welcome had shown itself to be sincere and had lasted through the year. She had done well in her music. Everyone praised her voice. What was it? Alice had become dearer than ever to her in their correspondence. Mr. Curtis was so good to her. Ah! was that it? At the thought of him her heart throbbed. She knew that when he was there she was happiest and that when he had gone she was most restless. She knew that his approval of her voice meant more to her than the praise of her instructor. She never sang so well for other people as she sang for him. She found herself looking forward too eagerly to his occasional calls. But she convinced herself that it was only because she was a little homesick and he always drove away the blues. Then she could talk of Alice and find a ready listener.

But when she knew he was coming she finished her work in half the usual time. She was cross to the children if they interrupted her reveries. What should she wear, she queried. To be sure she had not much from which to choose, but she could put a fancy collar on her prettiest gown, and she could do up her hair more becomingly. Would he notice it, she wondered. She arranged her hair a half dozen times, decided which side looked the better and planned to sit so he would see that side.

Then she stopped to think. What was she doing? It was all foolishness. She was ashamed of herself. But no—she was plain at best. He came only from a sense of duty, she told herself at such times, and she must make that duty as pleasant as possible. Leland noticed a change in the girl. She seemed really growing pretty. How much good college life was doing her. Then his thoughts turned to Alice as the cause of it all.

Commencement week was coming fast, with all its festivities. Everybody was planning for it. So many visitors were coming. Commencement concert was to be *the* event.

In due time Frances Wallace received a note from Mr. Curtis, asking for her company. She did not hesitate to accept his invitation. She expected it. Of course he would ask her. As she finished the note of acceptance, the servant came to the door with the mail. She took it eagerly. It was time for a semi-weekly.

"What," she exclaimed aloud, "Harold coming! Yes," and she read on. "I find I have to make a short business trip down your way next week, and I've planned to be with you Tuesday and Wednesday." "Oh! its too good to be true," she cried in ecstasy. "What perfect bliss, and he'll be here for the concert! What luck I hadn't sent that note to Leland. I guess I'd best write another one." Then she grew sober for an instant. "But poor Leland. It's cruel to desert him now. I'm afraid he's learned to care for me. But this will open his eyes, and oh! how can I wait till Tuesday."

Meanwhile Curtis was awaiting Frances' reply. Hearing the small errand boy of the house coming down the hall to his room, he thought he might have the desired missive.

"I say, bub, did you bring me any mail?"

"Yes, one. Seems to me they come pretty often nowadays. I brought you one just like that yesterday."

"Well, what's it to you? Give it to me."

He snatched the letter hastily. It was postmarked "Auburn." "Funny, I must say, she should write so soon. H'm, it's just a note," he said as he tore it open.

My Dear,—

I haven't time to write but a line, but I have the jolliest news to tell. I've decided at the last minute to come down for commencement. Isn't that great? Now don't tell Leland, not one word. Won't it be a surprise, though! Meet me Tuesday P. M., dear. Good-bye till then.

With lots of love,

ALICE A——.

Auburn, Tuesday, the Fourteenth.

"How in thunder did this come to me? It must be meant for Miss Hampton. She must have mistaken the envelope in her excitement. Good joke. 'Don't tell Leland,' oh no. 'Won't it be a surprise though?'" and he laughed outright. "Tuesday, just in time for the concert. But mister! Hang it all, anyway! I've asked Frances to go. What in thunder shall I do! I can't break my date now. She hasn't accepted yet, but of course she will. I've got my foot in it now."

"Mr. Curtis," called his landlady, "here is a note for you."

"All right. Thank you," he replied, as he went to the stairs to get it. He recognized Frances' dashing hand at once. "I know just what she'll say without opening it," he thought. But he slowly tore it open. His expression changed from perplexity to amazement as he read:

My Dear Mr. Curtis,—

Let me thank you for your kind invitation to the concert, but a previous engagement makes it impossible for me to accept.

Most sincerely,

FRANCES WALLICE.

Wednesday, June fifteenth.

Curtis was puzzled. "I'd like to know what that means. I'd like to know who has asked her, or whom she'd go with but me," he thought, astounded. "But then, that let's me out all right. Yet I would like to know who has had the audacity to ask her."

Leland, being a Senior and a very important one, was so busy the next few days that he found it impossible to get around to see Frances, but everybody must know how busy he was, he thought.

Tuesday came at last. He found himself at the station early. Finally he heard the whistle and his heart beat fast. He watched the people closely. Then he caught sight of Alice. She seemed looking for some one and a shade of disappointment came over her face as she looked in vain. When she stepped off he rushed up with a twinkle in his eye.

"Well this is a surprise, Alice."

"Why Leland Curtis, how did you know I was coming? I didn't write to you, did I, and who told you?"

"Nobody told me but yourself."

"But I didn't tell you."

"No, you didn't mean to."

"Why, what do you mean, Leland?"

"Well, I imagine perhaps Miss Hampton didn't get her regular letter last week, and maybe I got two."

"You don't mean that I made a mistake in the envelope!"

"It would look that way to an outsider. But who cares? You're here now, dear, and its awfully good to see you, little girl."

Curious eyes and busy tongues were soon at work. The same eyes that saw Curtis there to meet a young lady, saw Miss Wallace there to meet a young man at an earlier train. What more was needed to send Dame Rumor stalking through the college town?

Alice took a few minutes to run up to see her friend. She was taken completely by surprise and an explanation was in order. Then came the usual messages from home and the innumerable questions about "the folks."

"But Emma, how pretty you look. It's done my little girl good to come to college," she said, giving her an affectionate kiss. "What were you reading?" she added, seeing a book in her hand. "This is one of Leland's, I know; it's an old favorite of his." Emma started and her face flushed. She had forgotten for the moment.

"But isn't he the dearest boy, Emma? Now say he is. You must love him too by this time," she ran on in her ardent, girlish way, too happy to notice any change in her friend. Emma faltered an instant, then she controlled herself at once. Alice should see nothing of her feeling. "Yes, he is very nice. Oh! you must be so happy," she broke out again passionately.

"I am, but he's waiting for me and I must go. But you haven't sung for me yet. Come now and sing, won't you? Why what's the matter, dear? Are you afraid to sing before Leland? You look as if I'd asked a most dreadful thing of you."

"Oh! I can't," she gasped. She choked at the thought of singing.

"Well, little girl, don't be so scared," said Alice, laughingly. "You'll sing for me some time, alone. Leland will think I'm never coming, so good-bye. Come and see me in the morning sure. But don't look so worried, dear. I didn't know you were so timid. You used to like to sing any time. But don't forget to-morrow morning," and with a hasty kiss she hurried down to Leland.

Emma stood silent where Alice had left her. She seemed dazed. It was all so sudden. Then she heard the sound of steps on the walk and she went to the window. Emma watched them, motionless, till they disappeared. Then she flung herself on the bed, and for a moment lay quite still, till suddenly her whole body shook with passionate sobs. She loved her friend. Why had seeing her so happy made her so wretched? She had thought if Alice were only there everything would be all right. But now she could deceive herself no longer. And oh! the hopelessness of it! What had she done? She had done nothing, he had done nothing. Why was it? She was utterly miserable. On plea of a sick headache she did not leave her room, and all efforts to persuade her to go to the concert failed.

No little comment was caused that night by the beautiful stranger with Mr. Curtis. Who could she be, and where was Frances Wallace?

"Where is Miss Wallace, Leland? I'm anxious to see her," said Alice, when they had taken their seats.

"I don't know, I haven't seen her yet."

"And where is Emma, I wonder? Surely, she wouldn't miss this."

"Oh no, she'll be here. She's been looking forward to this concert all spring. It's all she stayed over for."

Just then, glancing toward the door, he saw Frances enter, escorted by a handsome man, who seemed most devoted. The usher taking their tickets led them down the aisle straight to the row where Alice and Leland were sitting. Frances took the seat next Leland. She looked a little surprised, smiled and bowed, casting a hasty glance toward the occupant of the seat the other side of Curtis as she did so.

"This is a surprise," she said laughingly.

"Yes, a little. May I have the pleasure of introducing to you my friend Miss Aylesworth, Miss Wallace?"

"Miss Aylesworth, I'm happy to know you," she said cordially, "and let me introduce Mr. Pembroke, Miss Aylesworth and Mr. Curtis."

Just then great applause greeted the appearance of the star of the evening. But many eyes wandered away from the soloist and the gossips enjoyed a rare treat.

Her Cousin Rob.

THE shadows were beginning to stretch across the campus, deepening the chill of a pale October day. The wide-branching elms were almost stripped of their foliage; there was a narrow border of green grass on either side of the winding walks, but elsewhere, it was dry and brown. The buildings loomed up with a dreariness, rather deepened than relieved by the bare vines which still clung to their rough sides and trailed over their porticos. The tennis courts gave the same impression. The nets sagged dejectedly, and the half dozen students who had come out for a last play found it hard to withstand the general gloom.

"I say, you!" suddenly called out a little red-haired fellow, shivering in a light-colored tennis suit. "I'm going to quit. Tennis has lost its flavor. Freezing doesn't agree with it, nor with me either. Let's go home."

His opponent, a tall, thin young man, who wore spectacles and had a generally senior-like aspect, was searching in the grass at the other end of the court, for a ball.

"You're a lazy little Prep," he remarked without looking up. "If you'd hustle around you might get warm, to say nothing about making a decent play. Look at Hoag and Miss Burgess. That's what I call playing."

"Pooh!" retorted the Prep, scornfully. "They're too struck on each other to mind the weather. I'm in a perfectly conscious condition yet, thank goodness."

"No more than they," responded the other, picking up his coat from the grass. "Nothing spoony there; they're cousins."

"Cousins!" ejaculated the Prep. "You don't say! They don't take after the same ancestor, do they?"

"O come on to supper, Sonny," said the Senior with good natured indulgence. "What do you know about them? Hoag isn't all bad, or half, for that matter. His cousin tries to look after him, and it may do some good. He thinks a good deal of her, after a fashion."

The Prep strolled along, his hands in his pockets and his face screwed up into what might be termed a meditative expression. "I—don't—know," he remarked judicially, "I—don't—know." The Senior was seized with sudden and unexpected impatience.

"I'm glad you've found it out," he said sharply. "I was beginning to think you never would come to it. Please don't limit its general application."

The Prep appeared unmoved. "Yes," he said serenely, " I guess I didn't know. I guess it isn't Hoag who is struck." Conversation languished between the Senior and the Prep.

In the meantime, the young man and woman, designated as Hoag and Miss Burgess, had finished playing and were leaving the campus. Miss Burgess was speaking and her tone was very persuasive.

"Please come up Tuesday night, Rob. A Hallowe'en party comes only once a year. I've invited ever so many of your friends and you'll be sure to have a good time."

There was a shade of deep anxiety on Hoag's open countenance.

"I'd be delighted to go, you know that, Jessie. But my work—now don't laugh—it's just piling up."

Miss Burgess did laugh a little. "That's the first time I ever heard you make that plea," she said. "What's the matter? Examinations?"

"That's only one thing," he answered, ruefully. "You know you wanted me to join a society. Well, the boys have just insisted on my writing up things. And what's more, there's something I've got to have done next week, and," with a touch of pathos—"I'm so slow. But 'Gopher' Jones promised to help me if I'd come around there Tuesday night."

Miss Burgess spoke severely: "I know that 'Gopher' Jones won't help you do any writing on Hallowe'en. And he isn't the sort,"—she stopped suddenly,—"Robbie dear, won't you come up to my party?"

The expression on Hoag's face changed from anxiety to patient resignation.

"I'll come," he said, "even though I have to

study on Sunday to make up. I hate to do that, especially since I know you are so opposed to it. But they say Professor Richards looked over examination papers the Sunday after he went with you to the picnic."

"I know better," and Miss Burgess spoke decidedly. "But it wouldn't make any difference if he did. Why, if I should throw myself into Lake Como, that wouldn't be any reason why you should follow suit, would it?"

Her cousin smiled into her troubled eyes, hiding the mischief in his own under a look of bland sentimentality.

"I don't know," he said gently, "but I would, though."

The girl made a little gesture of despair.

"You tire me to death with your frivolity, and you know one can't be really angry with you. I'll tell you what, Rob," she said in a different tone, "if you will come to my party, I will help you with whatever you have to write. I would rather do it than have you go off with that Jones. I'll be at home to-morrow afternoon."

Hoag suddenly became enthusiastic.

"You're a brick, Jessie! You're a better writer than Jones, too. I'll go right over and tell him I won't need him. Here you are at home. Shall I come at three? All right. Here's your racket. Good by."

Miss Burgess paused an instant on the steps to catch a last glimpse of him as he went whistling down the street. One was often tempted to do that. Even the "down town" people, from the little kindergarten girls to the old negro who cleaned crossings, were his ardent admirers. This was sometimes a source of anxiety to Miss Burgess, but just now her gray eyes were very bright with approval. She, too, was attractive, but in a different way. Her face was rosy, and she smiled happily, as she went up the steps.

"He is a dear boy," she said to herself. "He likes to tease me. I believe he didn't intend to have anything to do with that horrible Jones."

But she was mistaken in at least one of her conclusions. Hoag was already on his way to the room of "Gopher" Jones. He found that illustrious gentleman scowling over a pile of

"Shall I come at three?"

magazines. He looked up as Hoag entered.

"Hello 'Kid!' Any developments?"

"Yes," answered Hoag. "I'm going to a Hallowe'en party up to my cousin's Tuesday evening."

Jones dropped his magazine.

"A lot you are! Leave us in the lurch at this late day when you know we depend on you for most of the writing!"

Rob sat down on the end of the study table, his hands in his pockets, the embodiment of good-natured indifference.

"This is rich," he remarked. "You take me into this as a great favor in the way of gaining experience and so forth, and now you hold me responsible for the whole thing. You *are* consistent, 'Gopher.'"

Jones began piling up his magazines. "You're fooling," he said. "When you feel like talking sense, come around. I'm busy now."

Rob still sat on the table.

"But I mean it!" he declared. "I am going to that party, but in return for the pleasure of my company, my cousin is going to help me with some writing I have to do. See?"

Jones stared at him. "You're an idiot. She won't do it."

"She will too. She promised."

"So much the more confounded idiocy. Why don't you give the thing away to the whole college? Go down and confide in Prex, he may be able to give you some valuable suggestions."

Hoag got down from the table.

"Shut up with your sarcasm. I know what I am talking about. She'll know I'm in it, of course, but she won't tell on me. And I tell you it's our only chance. I can't do a thing alone. It isn't a bad idea, either,—rather novel to have a girl like her in it."

Jones' scowl relaxed a little.

"Rather," he admitted. "But I'm afraid you're running a risk, old man."

"You needn't be afraid of getting into it," retorted Hoag, going toward the door. "But if you really feel timid and would like to get out of the business, I presume I can get some other girl to take your place." And he dodged down the stairway just in time to escape a Latin grammar from the hand of the irascible Jones.

Miss Burgess found her cousin waiting for her at three the next day.

"I am surprised," she declared, "and ever so curious to know what in the line of work can have such an attraction for you. I am not a bit sure I can help. It isn't a political paper, is it?"

"Not exactly," and Hoag smiled grimly. "I'm sorry, Jessie, but I can't tell you all about it, not till after it comes off anyway. It's a secret, you see. As far as I'm concerned, I'd be willing to have you know, but a fellow must keep his word to the others. Now don't look that way. All I want you to do is to write some verse, in fact, some epitaphs."

"Epitaphs! Rob Hoag! For whom, I'd be pleased to know?"

"O, for a number of people," answered Hoag, coolly, "a few of the Seniors, but mostly Faculty. It's just a joke. 'Twon't phase the Seniors or the Faculty either."

"I suppose the Faculty never go to society," suggested Miss Burgess, somewhat doubtfully.

"Never," and a look of mingled surprise and amusement flitted over Hoag's face.

"At any rate, I think they'd prefer your verse to Jones'."

The allusion to Jones had its desired effect· Miss Burgess forgot her misgivings, and was soon busy writing, and however dissatisfied she may have been with the result, her cousin was very much pleased and grateful as well.

"Truly, Jessie," he declared as he took his leave, "I don't know what I'd ever do down here without my cousin."

And Miss Burgess, tired and still burdened with a sort of doubtful feeling in the depths of her consciousness, decided that perhaps it was worth while after all. At least, she was one ahead of that horrible Jones.

Tuesday evening was warm and clear. "Just the right sort of an evening," more than one busy student might have been heard to murmur, as he looked away from his books out into the dimly lighted streets. It seemed to have been the right sort of an evening for

the party; at any rate even the hostess was
satisfied with the success of her undertaking,
and not a small element in her satisfaction
was the fact that her cousin was there, the
merriest and most entertaining of all her
guests. She even felt a little lenient toward
"Gopher" Jones, who, poor fellow, must go
out on his dark mission of removing gates and
overturning sidewalks without the cheering
presence of her cousin Rob.

For his part, Hoag was still very grateful,
and so attentive to her during the evening,
that the Senior came near losing his temper
for the second time. But nothing was to be
gained in that way, so he contented himself
with admiring her from the other side of the
fireplace as they sat around it, telling stories.

She was very quiet and he wondered, in a
sentimental fashion, what she was thinking of.
But it would not have consoled him to know,
for she was dreaming of her cousin, winning
group honors, graduating as valedictorian perhaps, and the president saying beautiful things
about him, while all his relatives were delight-
fully surprised and everyone was saying, "It

was Jessie's influence that did it."

She was still in a very happy frame of mind as she walked down the street to breakfast the next morning. An overturned sidewalk caught her attention.

"Rob didn't do it," she thought triumphantly. "I believe he is outgrowing such things anyway," and she remembered that whenever she had seen him lately he was hurrying across the campus or through the corridors with the energetic swing which betokens the busy student.

Her thought ran on,—"I wonder what they did do, they must have been planning something. I'll find out at the club." Her curiosity was thoroughly aroused as she entered the hall, for an unusal commotion could be heard in the dining-room.

"What is it?" she demanded as she entered. "Anything new?"

"Well, I should say so!" "Haven't you heard?" "Why, the greatest thing!" came from various directions. "They've buried the Faculty!"

"What! Where?" Miss Burgess gasped.

"Look at her!" laughed a bright-eyed Sophomore who succeeded best in being heard above the commotion. "Girls, she's going to dig them up. Don't worry, dear; this won't hurt them a mite; it's nothing compared with some of their previous experiences. You see there are little mounds, and tombstones on the mounds, and epitaphs on the tombstones. And I forgot to say that the mounds are in the north-east corner of the campus."

The Sophomore paused an instant for breath, and then went on. "Mr. Decker has been up there, and we're all going up right after breakfast. You're late, Jessie. Girls, pass her the milk. That's another thing you missed, Jessie. There was real cream on the top of that milk when I got here this morning. I poured it on my oatmeal and then kept it until the others came and could see it. But when Mr. Decker told his story, I ate my oatmeal and forgot all about the cream."

Miss Burgess began her breakfast, only half heeding the chatter, until a sentence caught her attention.

"That wasn't bad," the Sophomore was

saying, "about Prof. Dixon and his measurements. Not even a Hallowe'en joker would be very hard on him."

Miss Burgess looked up with a sudden vague uneasiness. The Sophomore met her questioning glance.

"Oh, you haven't heard it," she said. "Mr. Decker copied that for the benefit of the Freshmen over there who are studying astronomy. Here 'tis. I'll read it again:

'He measured the distance between the stars,
  The circumference of the sun,
But these measurements were naught to him,
  There were harder yet undone.
So the depth of the average student's mind
  The old hero tried to sound;
The shock was too great, he measures now
  But four by six of ground.' "

"Oh say! read the other one!" demanded a sad-faced youth from the opposite side of the table. "That's a sight better. I could listen to it all day and only mourn that it's too good to be true. Whoever the author of those lovely lines may be, I tell you his soul is akin to mine. And I'm willing to wager my next piece of pie that his suffered the same hard-

ships mine did in the last chem. exam. Now
just read that lyric again.''

"I don't know whether I'd better or not,"
answered the Sophomore. "It seems to be
the means of developing a very bloodthirsty
spirit in your hitherto gentle nature. But if
you'll try to calm yourself, I'll read it to Miss
Burgess. Jessie, listen to these 'lovely lines,' ''
and the Sophomore read in tragic tones:

"Here lies the cold remains of him who with
    great fervor taught
That atom clings to atom, that every one is
    fraught
With power to clutch each other, to rend, and
    e'en to save
Some smaller, weaker atom, from a weaker
    atom's grave.
He joyed in fumes sulphurous, in smoke and
    ghastly puff
Of acid eating acid, till it eaten had enough;
So since he's left these realms of light, in
    midst of curdled gloom,
Old Pluto hath his dwelling fixed and fur-
    nished up his room.''

"Oh, ecstasy! ecstasy!" murmured the sad-
faced student. "Would that I could have had
a hand in it! Here, Barnes!" he called out,

with sudden revival of spirit, to a young man
about to leave the room, "if you're going
down town, just step into Thompson's and order a nickle's worth of forget-me-nots to be
sent up to the college cemetery, at my charge.
There's nothing small about me when my feelings are concerned."

The buzz of conversation went on as before,
but Miss Burgess didn't say a word. She felt
her face flame; her toast choked her; and she
was exceedingly thankful when she was left
alone in the dining room with injunctions to
hurry. She hoped that they would go and
leave her, but they did not, so she went with
them to the campus, dreading to attract their
attention to herself by refusing to go.

It was worse than she had anticipated, for
quite a crowd was already on the campus.
They were gathering around a little open
space beyond the tennis courts, where could be
seen the black mounds with their conspicuous
headboards. The epitaphs were written on
paper tacked to the boards.

It was with anguish of soul that Miss Burgess listened to the reading of the epitaphs

and the laughing and talking which accompanied it. Near her the Sophomore's voice rang out with,—

"Professor Snow in this mound below,
A director of youthful ideas.
'Neath a green coverlid is the dear fellow hid,
Nevermore to be able to see us.
His demise is sad, but there's nothing to add
Of 'mysterious dispensations,'
We must say for truth's sake, that he took,
    by mistake,
One of his own examinations."

"Didn't they honor Prexy!" came from another direction. "His is the only Latin one in the lot. My! but wouldn't the shades of the old poets have groaned if they had passed this way last night!"

"Lugete, O Veneres Cupidinesque,
Noster Princeps sepultus est sub terra.
Nos luximus dum vobis cum hic vixit,
Justum est nunc ut *vestri* ocelli rubent."

Miss Burgess suddenly turned. The sound of a very familiar voice came from a group of young men behind her.

"Impudent, aren't they?" one of them was

saying. "Wonder who did it. Bet 'twas the town boys."

She waited to hear no more, but with a sudden feeling of vindictiveness she walked away across the campus.

"He might have staid away," she said to herself, "at least while I was there." Her mind was in a tumult. What would they all think of her if they knew! She, Jessie Burgess, an upper classman, and at the head of some half dozen organizations. All at once she heard steps behind her. Her first thought was of her cousin. "I could choke him," she muttered under her breath and walked on as fast as she could. The one who followed gained on her, and almost caught up with her, but she would not look at him.

"Miss Burgess," he said.

She turned sharply. It was the tall, dark Senior. Her face flushed painfully.

"I didn't think,—I thought it was Rob," she stammered and then she wished she had said anything else. He seemed to take no notice of her embarassment, however, and began talking about the tombstones. "They are making quite an exciting thing out of it," he said, "but it will all blow over by night. The Faculty won't pay any attention to it—just a boyish prank. And the epitaphs are exceptionally mild—shows that the one who got them up isn't a real rowdy. A harmless trick, I call it."

Then he talked on about other things, never giving her time to say a word until he left her at the corner, half laughing, half crying.

"The great goose!" she said to herself as she went on alone. "He thinks Rob did it and wanted to comfort me. What *would* he say if he knew!"

She started early to chapel that morning to avoid the company of the other girls of the house, who were still talking about the epitaphs. By doing so, she met President Dean on the campus and was obliged to walk to chapel with him. He waited an instant for her, and as she joined him, he lifted his hat so courteously, and beamed upon her so approvingly, that her cup was quite full.

"Have you seen our little cemetery up here?" he asked after his brusque "Good morning," and then laughed heartily at her evident embarrassment as she stammered a reply.

"We don't care," he said good-naturedly. "Some one has wasted a lot of energy, that's all. Mark my word, if I wanted to find the author, which I don't, I would look among the E's. Students who get such reports as yours, Miss Jessie, don't have time for such nonsense."

And he thought her extremely modest as he glanced at the scarlet face.

It seemed to her that chapel would never be over that morning. To her distorted imagination the tutor in Greek had hung about his youthful neck a white slab, with "Bless our Baby" upon it, while a red and green halo surrounded the head of the senior philosophy Professor.

When chapel was over, she walked quickly away, looking neither to right nor left, but again she was overtaken, and this time it was Hoag. He greeted her cheerfully and then presented in an awed tone the all-prevailing question:

"Have you seen them?"

Miss Burgess neither looked at him nor replied, but he talked on, volubly.

"Great shame, isn't it? I'd like to know who did it. What do you suppose they'd do to him if they found out? My! he must have had cheek! Oh, do you recite here? Good-by."

That was not all. Hoag met her a dozen times in the next few days, always with a remark ready.

"Do you remember that verse about Prof. White? Wasn't it audacious?" or, "That epitaph keeps ringing in my ears."

He tired of it after a little and everyone else ceased to speak of the affair, but Miss Burgess could hardly forget it. She treated her cousin with a steady coolness which that young man found quite depressing. One morning near the close of the term, he found her in the library, and went up to her with a most lugubrious countenance.

"Cousin Jessie," he said, "I am going into a decline. The rigor of the climate is too much for me. And, Jessie, as a last request,

will you write an epitaph for me? I don't
care about your flattering me much, but I
wish you'd say that toward the last I repented
my former wickedness and tried to be honest.
Please be thinking about it, for I may need it
soon.''

Strange to say, instead of being angry, she
forgave him immediately.

The Senior, who soon discovered the changed
relations, was magnanimous enough to say that
he was glad of it.

"None of the rest of us thought it was so
bad," he said, "but you, being a young
woman with a very high standard of honor,
and Rob's cousin, may have looked at it from
a little different standpoint.''

She replied meekly that perhaps she did.

II.

PORTRAITS.

Jack Dumbaugh.

EVERY fellow who had been in college for six weeks knew Jack Dumbaugh. He had the reputation of being "queer," not obtrusively so, but enough to make him a subject of frequent comment. The first day he came to town in the fall of 189—, "Big" Crane, the captain of the 'Varsity, was at the station with the manager of the team, on the lookout for any promising candidates. As Jack swung off the train, the two watchers spied him and, going up, introduced themselves. After giving him some pointers as to rooms, Crane asked Jack, commenting on the fact that he was well built and sinewy, whether he had ever played foot-ball. Although forced to admit that he had not, Jack said that 'he would be willing to come out and practice for a while at least, but being a new man, he supposed that he would not make much of a showing the first season.'

He found a room in the central part of the
town, as near the business portion as the students were allowed to live, and picked up as his
room-mate a sophomore, Fred Durnham. He
registered Junior, but to all the students' in-
quiries as to where he had prepared for that
class, he would only reply that he had been
for two years in a small college in his own
state, Ohio. Contrary to his expectations, he
exhibited a good deal of skill in foot-ball,
gaining a position as sub-end, but as "Spike"
English, who played tackle on Jack's side,
used to put it, "You can't depend on Dumbaugh; sometimes he will get in and break up
the interference as quick as a flash, but at
other times he won't get started until the half
has got clear to him, and he can't touch the
interference." Still, although he would surprise and delight the spectators by his occasional brilliant plays, he was by no means pop-
ular among the boys. For he was always in a
serious mood, sometimes even irritable when
the coach pointed out the mistakes he had
made in practice, though he invariably apolo-
gized later for his hot temper. He was a good

student, but his instructors were unable to understand him, for although he paid the strictest attention, as soon as he had recited, he seemed to have no further interest in the class, and often what interest he did exhibit was mechanical.

There sprang up a strange friendship between Jack and his room-mate. Fred Durnham was a jolly, impulsive young fellow, always on the lookout for something to get him into trouble; but he thought a great deal of Jack. Often when he would come into the room after some lark, and find Jack settled back comfortably in a rocker studying or gazing vacantly at the ceiling, he would imagine that he was homesick, and would give him a long account of the boys' doings, trying to induce him to join the crowd in some of their fun. Jack never seemed to be troubled by these interruptions, however, but when Fred had finished, he cautioned him about going too far and getting sent home. The only social affair which Jack attended, was the annual reception given by the senior girls to the foot-ball team. When "Big" Crane first told him about the reception, Jack utterly refused to go, declaring he could not be hired to attend any of those dress affairs; but upon Crane's representing to him that the girls had planned on a certain number being present, and that it would upset all their arrangements unless he went, he relented. Instead of proving hard to be entertained, Jack was very much of a success as a listener, and established himself readily in the good graces of his hostesses. Fred was delighted at the reports he heard, and thought that Jack was going to reform immediately. Yet after this event he drew back into his shell again, and hardly went out of the house except to his meals and recitations.

The junior class decided to present Hamlet during the spring term, instead of publishing the regular Junior Annual, and every member of the class felt that Dumbaugh was the man to take the leading role, but Jack again refused to accept any position which would make him prominent. Night after night, Ray Howell, the manager of the play, came over to his room and reasoned with him. Finding

that no personal appeal would persuade Jack,
he tried a different line of argument. "Why,
it isn't that you keep yourself from getting a
reputation, Jack—you don't care a snap for
that, I suppose—but the class needs you.
You have an entirely different temperament
from any of the other fellows, and you would
be just suited to represent Hamlet." "Well,"
replied Jack, with a good deal of spirit,
"there have been many Hamlets in this world,
men who have suffered from just such doubts
and struggles as he did; but if you are certain
that I am best fitted to represent him, I'll try
it."

The weekly rehearsals began about the first
of March, and by the last of April, the parts
had been well committed. Although satisfied
that he had made the best selection of characters, Howell was often perplexed as he
watched Jack. One week he would put the
most intense meaning into his words, the
next, he seemed as far away from the play as
though he were reciting a passage from some
comedy. "I do wish I could make that fellow
out," he said to the trainer. "I know that

he has the right part, and he probably will
make a success of it, but there is something
the matter with him, and I can't find out
what it is. You can't rely on him for any
length of time whatever." The final dress
rehearsal, the afternoon before the play, was a
sorry time for the actors. Jack was unable to
go through with his part at all creditably.
He did not make himself heard half way
across the room, and even made a few slight
omissions. Howell was in despair.

Evening came and the house was packed.
It was not a large building, eight hundred filled
it comfortably, but to-night fully a thous-
and had crowded the ground floor and the
one small gallery, half an hour before the play
was advertised to begin. The front seats were
reserved, according to the usual custom, for
the Seniors, but with this exception the crowd
was very much mixed. The students were almost all there, and jolly couples scattered
through the audience were discussing the
play and the actors. Directly back of the
Seniors were several of the older citizens of
the town, who had come to join the students,

and lose themselves in the happiness and eagerness of the younger part of the audience. The stage and gallery draped with Old Gold, and the yellow tulips of the ushers gave evidence of the class spirit and interest. As they passed back and forth trying to crowd chairs down the aisles for those standing in the rear of the building, they heard many comments on the rehearsals and the prospects for the play.

"Oh, Mr. Crane," said Miss Eldredge, the freshman belle of the college, to the sedate Senior at her side, "do you think that Mr. Dumbaugh will make a failure to-night? The girls were saying that he couldn't do a thing this afternoon, and wouldn't it be perfectly dreadful if he should spoil it now!"

In one corner of the room, far back under the gallery, sat an old couple, the parents of one of the actors.

"No, Mary," said the father, "I don't believe in sending Lafe off to school to learn no acting. I would rather have kept him ter home on the farm with me, but he is most through now, and he has behaved himself pretty well, so I guess we won't say nothing about this."

"I wouldn't, John," she replied, "Just think how hard Lafe studies, and you know he is taking this instead of foot-ball this spring. He promised me he wouldn't put on one of them suits all this term if I would let him go into this."

"What a creditable sacrifice Lafe Tenant is making," said a mischievous youth behind the old couple to his companion, "but I suppose the folks appreciate it."

All unconscious of the mirth her remark had created, the fond mother was straining her eyes to catch the first glimpse of her son. The scene on the curtain, a street in Venice, proved a source of interest to some of the audience. The slender gondolas and the picturesque gondoliers were variously commented upon, but even with this diversion time passed slowly for the anxious crowd.

At last the college orchestra was through with the Danube Waltzes and the curtain rolled slowly up. The stage was small, although the scenery had been skillfully arranged so that the action did not reveal how cramped the players really were. During the first scene the mass of people below seemed expectant and uneasy, but when Jack came upon the stage, an almost painful silence came over them as they listened for his first words, uttered slowly and penetrating to the farthest part of the building. "A little more than kin and less than kind." His voice and manner were in perfect unison with the character he was portraying, and as Howell heard him, he congratulated himself again on his selection.

As soon as the first act was over, Jack hurried to a dressing room and locked the door. Then he took from his pocket a small hypodermic syringe and three white tablets. These he crushed in his palm, and drawing a syringe full of water from a tumbler on the window, he slowly dropped it on the powder until it was dissolved. Then taking the solution up again into the syringe, he inserted the hollow needle into his bared arm, injected the contents, and withdrew the instrument. After holding his finger for a moment over the puncture in his arm, he hastily drew down his sleeve and started for the door. Just as he unlocked it and stepped out into the passage-way, he ran into Fred, who had come up to congratulate his room-mate.

"Hello, old man!" burst out the joyful youth, slapping him on the shoulder, "I've been looking everywhere for you; where have you been hiding? Why, you are altogether too modest. I never thought that I'd see you turn such an actor as you are to-night. Some scamp was telling me that you had lost your nerve this afternoon, but he is singing a different tune now." Jack listened to his enthusiastic greeting with a smile, but had to hasten back to the stage without making any reply. "Well, that man Dumbaugh is a surprise," was the comment that Fred heard as he edged his way back to his seat. "How natural his acting is!"

In the closing scene, the audience was hushed with deep feeling as Jack challenged Laertes to renew the contest, and, with a thrill of triumphant joy, accomplished on the king his long-sought revenge. When the curtain fell, Fred again hurried back to the dressing-room, where he met Jack before, and found him sitting on a table listless and utterly exhausted. From the stage could be heard the merry voices of the Juniors as they greeted one and another of the actors, and soon there were loud calls for Dumbaugh. As he heard his name, Jack roused up a little, and telling Fred that he was too tired to see anyone, they went out by the stage entrance, and hurried home. Here Jack threw himself upon his bed, and with instructions to Fred to let no one disturb him, fell into a troubled sleep. To the fellows who came around to see Dumbaugh, Fred explained that he was very tired and had gone to bed, asking that no one disturb him. All the next day Jack lay in a dazed condition. He refused to let Fred send for a physician, assuring him that he was all right, only very much worn, but insisted on his keeping everyone out. Toward night he came over to the table where Fred was studying, and threw himself into the rocker, where he sat in silence for several minutes, looking around the room. Finally he said, "Fred, I got a letter from an uncle out West the other day, asking me to come out there and live with him. I know the fellows will quiz you, so I won't tell you just where I am going, but I shall never be back again. I thought I had better say nothing about this before the play, as it would only trouble you; but my uncle told me to come as soon as possible, and I wrote him that I would start to-night, so I am going to pack up my things, and go on the eleven o'clock 'flyer.' Please inform the President to-morrow, but tell him that you know nothing definite about my destination, and do not understand my purpose in leaving. But above all never say a word to any of the boys about this.''

To all Fred's entreaties to wait a day or two, Jack would only reply that he could not disappoint those who were expecting him. There was a determined look on Jack's face which Fred had not seen there before, so he did not say another word, but thinking that Jack had some trouble which he could not tell, he almost reproached himself for being so selfish that even his room-mate would not make a confidant of him. At half-past ten the two

bove all, never say a word to any of the boys
about this."

boys went down to the depot. Fred was afraid to trust himself to say anything. As the train was pulling out Jack caught his room-mate's hand in a firm grip and said: "Fred, you have been a true friend to me. If I can I'll write you. God forgive me if I have done you any harm." Then the train was off and Fred stood watching it till he could no longer distinguished the two red lights at the rear.

The next morning Fred went to the President and told him that Dumbaugh had left school, without giving any explanation of his action. As soon as Jack's departure was known, the most intense interest was aroused, and a great variety of theories was adduced to explain it. About a week later a group of boys were gathered in Fred's room discussing the topic they could not drop from their thoughts.

"I'll bet you," said "Nick" Trevers, "that Dumbaugh had a girl somewhere around, and he got so homesick that he couldn't stand it; so after his success here, he thought he'd go and tell her about it; ten to one it was back in Ohio where he went to school."

"Yes, he did act like a love-sick looncy, didn't he," added Bartlett. "You couldn't get him to look at a girl once a fortnight."

"No," interjected Crane, "that man had something more than love affairs on the brain. I have played foot-ball four years, and I know that when a man acts as Dumbaugh did occasionally, there is something more serious the trouble with him. But I can't see through it."

After they had gone, Fred sat down in Jack's old rocker, and took from his pocket a letter already worn, which, with a heavy heart, he read once more.

Denver, Col., May 21st, 189—.

Dear Fred:—

I must tell you my whole story so that you can understand my actions at school and my reasons for leaving, for I am sure that you never suspected anything of what I am going to tell you.

My grandfather was an habitual user of morphine and died from the effects of the habit. My father, however, although he inherited the desire for it, had sufficient moral courage to resist; but I had not, and began to use it when I was fifteen. Just before my eighteenth birthday, father heard that I was using the drug, and he was so angry that he would not let me live in the house. He promised me $500 a year, and more, if I needed it, but told me to go somewhere and get rid of my cursed habit. I thought that I had plenty of will-power and could do it easily, so, as I told you, I went to a college near home for two years, but did not dare go home, for I could not break myself of the habit entirely, though using smaller and smaller quantities. On the advice of a physician, I made a change at the close of the two years, thinking that, by so doing, I might get some strength. Last fall I used very little of the drug but occasionally before a game, I would take enough to brace me up. When I came to the play, the strain was too great, and I had been taking morphine regularly, since the re-hearsals began. Just before the play, I took a heavy dose, enough, as I thought, to influence me during the evening, but after the first act I felt weak and had just taken more when you found me in the dressing-room. Then I realized that if I stayed there much longer, I would become so dependent upon it that my use of it must be discovered, and I decided to come out here to a private sanitarium in charge of an old friend of my father's. The story about my uncle was, as you will see, en-

tirely fictitious, but I could not tell you the
awful truth. I am doing as well as possible.
The physician says that there is a good chance
of my getting entirely cured of the habit, although he has seldom treated anyone who began to use morphine as young as I did. At
any rate I believe it is my last hope. Don't
tell any of the fellows, for I can't bear to have
them know how weak I am. It will not do
any good to trace me, for if I do get well I
shall stay out here; but don't forget me, Fred.
I didn't intend to write you such a long letter, but I have never before bared my soul to
anyone, and I can trust you,

Your sincere friend,

JACK DUMBAUGH.

For a long time Fred sat staring at the letter in his hand, thinking of the comments the
boys had made, but at last he spoke fiercely:
"Why couldn't he have told us! We might
have helped him."

Then he twisted the letter up, and touching
a match to it, threw it into the grate, while
to his mind there came, "The heart knoweth
his own bitterness."

In the Fall of the Year.

THE lengthening shadows fell upon the little town of Herndon in quite the usual manner, but this evening the pulse of life seemed to throb a little faster than it had for several months, for the summer sleep of the college town was over.

All day the busy students had been hurrying along the shady streets, back and forth from the campus to the various houses which for nine months in the year they call home. In the changing crowd of gay young people there was talk of registration, new teachers, new clubs, and all those innumerable things which have a part in the annual settling of the students. Sometimes there was an exchange of vacation experiences and a few words of regret over some friend or classmate who had not returned. But that was among those students to whom the broad, straight streets were familiar; who knew the hitching-post at which old

(95)

Jennings' apple-wagon was always tied when he was in town. They knew too who those orthodox people were who had not as yet abandoned the fences about their homes. Yet even the old students spoke for the most part of the new year just opening, and altogether they gave a sense of thorough awakening and newness of life to the streets, shaded by the green arch of maple, locust and cotton-wood trees.

In a large, well-kept, shady yard, surrounding a rambling brick house on College street, an old gentleman sat at a rustic table, which he had moved from its usual place on the porch to a bench under the great elm tree. More than one group of passing students had looked in longingly at the cool, inviting shade, but the Professor had placed his bench where a large clump of lilac and snow-ball bushes screened it from the street, so, for the most part, he was unnoticed. Scattered all about him were books and papers, for he had tried to busy himself through the warm afternoon, working over his translation of Paul's epistles. But as he sat there writing or turning the

leaves of his reference books, there was an air
of dejection in the attitude of the bent figure,
and too often, with his gray head thrown
slightly back, he gazed absently up the street.
Any one seeing his face once would have felt an
impulse to look again. For though worn and
wrinkled, it had those deep, clear, gray eyes in
which the soul so often appears. Experience
of the noblest kind was written there, yet to-
day a shadow rested on that usually placid
face, for this man was passing through a new
and sobering experience.

For more than a score of years he had been
connected with the college up the street. He
had filled the chair of Greek, and watched the
rapid development of the school with the
deepest interest. Having that temperament
which drives a man whole-souled into the thing
nearest, he had given his best life to the
building up of this college. But now his part
in the activity of it all was over. He had intended to extend his vacation into October,
but when the second week in September came,
he was back in Herndon. He belonged here.
He could not stay away.

A crowd of students passed down the street, keeping time to a lively march which they were whistling. They made a gay company as they swung along, followed by the college mascot, a ragged poodle, decorated with the college colors. A good-natured townsman passed them and said, laughing:

"Here, don't paint the town too red, boys. Not all of a sudden." But he added to himself, "They don't know how much good it does us all to have 'em back." Then looking in toward the brick house, "I wonder if Mitchell doesn't feel a little lost these days."

The lines in Professor Mitchell's face deepened as he looked after the boys, and he pushed his work from him impatiently. But in doing so he shoved one of the books off the table. It was the Bible and, smiling at his own bitter thoughts, the Professor leaned forward to pick it up. As he did so his eye caught the words on the open page, "But now having no more place in these parts—". He closed the book almost roughly, but opened it again half unconsciously, trying to find the same line, while he asked himself once more:

"Can I ever be satisfied to stop and stagnate while all the work goes on? Why must I?" Then in answer to the thought, "They also serve who only stand and wait," he exclaimed aloud: "That is hardly twentieth century philosophy. But it is over now, and yet—if I could only feel that after all it had really been of any use!" and the gray head sank a little lower.

Suddenly he was conscious that a party of students had stopped on the corner opposite. Turning towards the street, he heard the enthusiastic voice and saw the bright face of a blonde girl in the conventional blue blazer. She was facing the setting sun and saying in a clear voice: "How lovely! I'm so glad I made you stop to look. Do you always have such sunsets in Herndon?"

"That is fine," admitted the short dark fellow who had been her companion as they came up the street. "I suppose they would all pass, Miss Taylor, if one ever had time to look at them. But you'll soon have something else to do."

Owens, being a Sophomore, considered this

to be the correct way to impress new students. However, the little blonde did not seem to be impressed, but went on with what Owens considered the naïve rapture of the unsophisticated. Still he smiled assent for she was such a pretty girl, and she made a lovely picture of youthful enthusiasm as she stood a little apart from her companions, gazing down the wide, shaded street, where the glorious light of the Iowa sunset was turning the leaves to gold, and making the arc lights gleam like balls of fire. Out beyond the tree-bordered street, she saw the broad prairie, rolling out to meet the splendor of the western sky, a molten mass of colors shading into opal tints, and the indescribable beauty of the sunset glow enchanted her. But Professor Mitchell looked with admiration at the girl as she stood there in the reflected light, her slight figure so full of life, and not till she turned again to her companions did he resume his work, letting his fingers beat a nervous tattoo on the edge of the table.

While Leonore Taylor and Frank Owens had been discussing the sunset, a girl wearing the

scarlet badge of the Reception Committee had
tried to entertain the other member of the
party—young Taylor, who was getting his first
impressions of Hawkeye. She was chatting
about the Y. M. and Y. W. C. A. reception
and what the prospects were of knowing any
one on Monday whom you had met Saturday
night. But at the same time she had been
watching the progress of a tall fellow in a
gray suit, who was coming rapidly down the
street toward them. Now she stepped forward to meet him and offered her hand with a
bright smile, saying: "Mr. Berry, I'm very
glad to see you. When did you get back?"

"I came down on the Central just now.
Think every one came down on that train or
met it. There was a bigger jam than usual.
I looked for you but didn't see you; supposed
you were piloting some new people, so—"

"You remind me! We have two new Freshmen here and are on our way to supper. I'll
introduce you."

As they turned to the others the Senior and
Sophomore shook hands so heartily that Taylor, the new Freshman, wished he was not

quite so new. But he felt better when, after the introductions, Owens said: "This is Dick Maxwell's friend, who is going to do something for us in athletics." And the Senior turned on him an interested and approving stare, saying, "Oh, yes! Dick wrote me about your coming down. We need all you new men and we'll count on your filling Dick's place." Then to the others, "What's the discussion?"

"Nothing, only Mr. Owens was trying to show Herndon scenery to our protégés instead of taking them to supper. I suggest we go on."

"Well, Frank needn't be in too much of a hurry about showing off our scenery. We may have what some one called, 'The splendid scenery of the sky,' but as Miss Kimball said last year, 'People generally find no trouble about taking in most of the scenery around here during their first year.' You can appreciate the fine irony of that remark later in the year, Miss Taylor."

Then the party strolled up the street, but were stopped directly opposite the lilac bushes by a boyish looking, blue-eyed youth, who appeared suddenly amid a great racket of whirring wheels, bicycle bell and a wild-cat whistle. He leaned his wheel against a convenient tree and, after politely doing his duty to the others of the party, threw himself impulsively on the Senior. Berry put one arm around him and patted him on the head as he said:

"Well, well, Clark! I wondered that the omnipresent Prep hadn't appeared before. Oh there now, don't look so injured. It is a Freshman. And just think, you won't have a chance to exercise that pull you used to brag about so modestly. How many new Profs there are! Have you met any of 'em?"

By this time the ex-Prep had wriggled away and composed himself. But now he made a wry face, struck an attitude and answered:

"Not I! I'll put off the evil day as long as possible."

But Berry was looking in toward the brick house and at last he said:

"Really, people, talking about new Profs, I can't help thinking about what we have lost and what these new people have missed."

"Now I say," groaned Clark, "what have
we done to deserve this,—and so soon? I see
he is about to mount his hobby and his 'high
seriousness' is more than I can bear. I beg to
be excused." And with an all-including wave
of his cap, he swung himself upon his wheel
and departed as hastily as he had come.

They all laughed as they looked after him
and the Senior would have followed him, but
Miss Taylor exclaimed:

"Oh tell us about your hobby any way!
What or whom have we missed?"

Berry smiled and said:

"Clark always groans over my extreme admiration for Professor Mitchell. But he can't
say anything against him. You ought to hear
him try! It's all his way. He really thinks
just as I do. Prof lives in here," turning his
head toward the brick house. "Used to be
the Greek Professor. He has been here a long
time and has just about half made the college.
He has influenced more students and done
more real good than any one man I ever knew.
What I was thinking was, that, though the
new Prof may teach the 'Freshies' to scan

Homer, etc., in quite the same way, it will be a long time before we find anybody who will teach the 'Menschen-Liebe' that he used to throw in. You'll never know just what you missed by not coming before his day was over."

As Berry paused almost out of breath after his outburst of "high seriousness", Gertrude Manning said:

"Oh don't say 'his day is over' in that tone. Of course we're all sorry to have him quit active work, but think of the spirit he has put into old Hawkeye. Haven't you ever noticed that the very books he has put into the Library with those 'exam' fees, which he always looked apologies for collecting, are full of him—the things he loved best? He didn't always buy for his own department either! And, as you said yourself, he has influenced so many people. His day isn't over!"

"Well I guess you're right, Gertrude,—you mostly are. At least I'd better say so now, for between the sunset and an argument our friends won't get their supper. The sight of Clark has reminded me that I promised to

meet some fellows down town at six, and I'm
late now. Bring Taylor over to the room after
supper, Frank; the new coach is going to be
there and I want the fellows to meet him."
And tipping his gray cap he was off down the
street whistling "Co-ed."

It had been only a little thing, this meeting
on the corner. But as the students walked up
toward the "club," the tea-bell rang in the
brick house, and the old man, who mounted
the steps in answer to its summons, looked
satisfied.

Brainard's Transformation.

PAUL BRAINARD was probably about as conceited a person as anyone whose name had been entered on the Registrar's books since the founding of Hawkeye College. In truth his conceit was colossal. But in the second semester of his sophomore year a change came over him, and when it was seen that the change was permanent it became a much mooted question, what had caused Brainard's transformation.

It happened in this way. It was Thursday noon. The daily grind was again over, and as he had been more than usually fortunate in escaping flunks that forenoon, he was enjoying to the fullest extent the bracing February air in the bright sunshine, as he walked from the campus to his room. He was not enough of a philosopher to define his view of life, but if he had been able to put it into words it would have been found that he considered an indefinite

(107)

something given to him, out of which he was proposing to get a maximum of pleasure with a minimum of effort. And so it was entirely in accordance with his nature that, as he passed along the street, he should feel that all the beauties of this winter day were intended principally for his benefit; and also that it should suddenly strike him, as it often did, that he was a pretty good sort of a fellow, take him any way you pleased. He drew his shoulders back, tilted his cap a little more to one side, in order that his black curls might show to a better advantage, and smiled from pure joy in his own personal appearance. He wished that he might meet that junior girl who had so deliberately "bagged" him at the time of the last lecture, and he resolved to go into Chapel late the next morning to attract her attention to his good looks. So impressed was he with his own importance, that he failed to recognize a Prep, whom he met at the foot of the stairs leading to his room; and the Prep was so very young and inexperienced in the ways of the college world, that he considered this lack of notice as the thing to be ex-

pected as a matter of course from all college
men.

Brainard mounted the stairs, entered his
room, and throwing his overcoat, hat and
books on a couch sank into a willow chair with
a sigh of content. He and his room-mate, Bob
Newbold, occupied a room in a house not far
from the campus and it was furnished with
rather more elegance than is usual in a boy's
room in a Western college town.   As he sat in
his easy chair, he surveyed the room approvingly.   In the center of a Turkish rug stood
a small table, upon which lay a couple of
meerschaum pipes, a box of Yale Mixture,
several copies of *Munsey's*, a hand-mirror, and
a deck of cards. At one end of the room hung
dark brown chenille curtains which half hid
the bed and the bureau, and upon which were
pinned various souvenirs of class parties with
concert and field-day programs.   The walls
were covered with photographs, half-tones of
the college athletic teams, and snap shots of
various scenes of college life, while twined
around all were the college colors, giving a
touch of brilliancy to the otherwise dull back-

ground. In a corner stood a couple of tennis rackets and a guitar also decorated with the college ribbons, while in every chair, on the couch, and on the floor near the window, were pillows of all shapes, sizes, and stuffing. To Brainard these were closely associated with some of the faces looking down from the walls, most of them being gifts from some of his "old girls". His glance wandered across to the opposite corner where his room-mate's desk stood, and he vaguely wondered why Bob did not put some of his pictures on the wall instead of sticking them in pigeon-holes, entirely forgetting that he himself had so monopolized the wall space that there would be no other alternative, than to sky them like the work of unknown artists at the exhibitions. He looked at his watch, and finding that it was already past dinner time, he jumped up hastily and started to put on his overcoat; but as he turned around an unopened letter lying on his desk attracted his attention. Crossing over quickly he picked it up. He saw that it was from his mother and, opening carelessly, he read:

Wapello, Wednesday, Feb. 11, 189—.

My Dear Paul:—

I have not heard from you for some time, but I know that you are so busy with your studies that your time is limited. I, too, am very busy but I think of you every day, and often wish I might run in now and then and see you. We have just had a very heavy fall of snow, the trees in the yard are drifted full, and the branches bend under the load. It makes me think of the times when you were a little boy, and used to enjoy, so much, shovelling paths and building snow houses in the drifts.

I received some very sad news this morning, which also made me think of your boyhood and your playmates. I heard only a little while ago that Laura Gardner was dead. She died at about one o'clock this morning. Her death was entirely unexpected, as she had been ill but a few days, with what was supposed to be intermittent fever but which the doctors now think to have been typhoid. I am very sorry for her poor mother. I will go over to-day to see her. Laura is to be buried on Friday, services at the church......

He could read no more. A torrent of recollections of his childhood poured in upon him, and crumpling the trembling paper in his hand, he turned to his easy chair, and sinking into it sat gazing out of the window at the house across the street.

As he gazed, his surroundings seemed to fade away and he found himself again living his boyhood. He saw again the quiet farmhouse, standing half-hidden by the trees, in the midst of the velvety lawn with its patches of sunlight and shadow. He could see the great, rambling barns with their hot, dusty mows filled to the eaves with the fragrant prairie hay; he could see the cool, shady grove, and the creek winding about under the willows, where the rippling water, the sighing wind, the rustling leaves, the far away, mournful coo of the turtle dove, the occasional drumming of the woodpecker, and the monotonous buzzing of insects, united to form a harmony and rhythm known to no other music than Nature's. He recalled the broad expanse of sky as seen from the meadow, whence, on summer evenings, one could watch the sun go down, and trace the almost imperceptible fading of color until only a few light-

tinged clouds were visible, where but a short
time before there had gleamed a crimson
glory. And into all these pictures of the past,
there came the face and form of a brown-
haired lassie—Laura—his playmate.

A flapping screen on one of the windows of
the house across the street caught his eye, and
he wondered why the people did not take
down their screens in the winter time or, if
they would leave them up, why they did not
at least fix them so that the wind could not
blow them about.   Then his thoughts drifted
back into reverie.

Playmates—yes—what happy times they had,
playing together day after day, running races
on the lawn until they were tired, and then
swinging in the hammock with the summer
breeze fanning their flushed cheeks. He remembered how on clear moonlight nights they
used to sit on the rustic bench under the big
evergreen, watching the stars and counting
the meteors, as they shot for a moment into
sight, and then disappeared into darkness; and
he seemed to hear again Laura's little scream
of delight whenever she saw one first. He

thought of the hide-and-seek in the barn on
rainy days; of the fun they had jumping from
the big beams into the soft hay; how once
Laura had slipped and fallen into a dark oat-
bin, and he had impetuously plunged in after,
where they remained in mutual terror until
rescued by one of the work-hands.   He
thought of the hot, sultry afternoons spent
under the willows by the bend of the creek,
building houses by packing the damp sand
around their bare feet, and constructing forts
garrisoned by companies of sticks, with corn-
cobs for cannon, and pebbles for ammunition.
He thought of their tent under the hemlock
trees by the big boulder, where they played at
being Indians, and feasted on dainties procured
by stealth from their mothers' pantries.   He
thought of the long tramps over the ⸱meadows
to the spring, gathering the beautiful wild
flowers,—tiger-lilies, phlox, and golden-rod—
to make bouquets to appease the wrath of
anxious mothers.

And this girl, just blooming into womanhood, with all the possibilties of a noble life
before her, was dead. Yes, dead! And it

seemed to break the last link between him and his own past. That sunny face glowing with health, was now ashen and cold; those laughing eyes were glazed. What did it mean?

For a long time he sat musing, lost in contemplation of the reality of death, brought home to him now as never before. His reverie was suddenly ended by the arrival of his roommate, who came rushing up the stairs, three steps at a time, and burst into the room with:

"Look a' here, you confounded idiot, what in the deuce 's the matter with you, that you didn't come to dinner?" And then seeing the letter, "Old man given you the g. b., eh?"

Paul looked up with a half smile and said, "No. Just got some bad news—girl I used to know died yesterday. Been dreaming I guess."

.   .   .   .

That afternoon he packed a few things in his grip and quietly announced to the astounded Bob, that he was going home on the evening train; that he didn't have to go; that Prex knew he was going and had excused him; and that he would be back in a few days. The latter in answer to questions.

A delayed train caused him to miss connections and prevented his arrival in time for the funeral. But the day after, he went over to the little cemetery on the bleak hill-side. The new-made grave showed distinctly, a black mound of earth standing out in marked contrast to the ghostly whiteness of the snow covered prairies. Crawling through the barbed-wire fence he made his way to it. All around, the trampled snow gave mute evidence of the good will of the country people toward Laura. For the day of the funeral had been dark, threatening and bitterly cold, and the tracks showed that many had braved the weather to witness the last sad rites.

There beneath a weight of frozen earth, lay the form of Laura Gardner, shut out from the warmth and comfort of life forever—forever—eternity. A shadowy conception of the vastness of the term began to steal over him and he began to see the insignificance of the individual and the omnipotence of the Infinite.

He began to see how men could "die every minute—forgotten—swept into heaps like autumn leaves, their lives mere soil and

" So he stood with bowed head —."

foothold for the generations that come after them."

And there in his soul he fought out a battle between the selfishness of his nature which had grown unconsciously, until it had become a part of himself; and altruism now for the first time became more than a mere word to him. Altruism, which commanded a recognition of the rights of others and a life devoted to their welfare. So he stood with bowed head until the dusk began to shade into darkness. Finally his meditation was broken by the jingle of sleigh-bells and the crunch of the runners cutting through the snow. After the sleigh had passed, he laid on the grave a sprig of holly, that Laura had loved so well, and then turned quickly away.

On Monday, after an affectionate farewell to his mother, he returned to college. All through the long journey, the throb of the engine, the rattle of the cars, the clickity-clack, clickity-clack of the wheels, seemed but an accompaniment to his reveries. He did not notice the sunless landscape, as it raced past the car windows, until he neared the college town. Then as he came in sight of the college buildings, there dawned upon him a fuller realization of the meaning of the change that had come over him, its relation to his daily life, and the difficulties he would have to meet in trying to live up to his new ideals. For a moment his decision wavered. It would be so much easier to go back and live the old life outwardly, justifying himself by his inward change for the better, and waiting for time to bring about the outward change. But it was only for a moment that he hesitated, for there came to him the memory of a new-made grave and a bleak, wind-swept hill-side, and with that memory, the battle he had fought there. He left the train with a stronger resolution than before, to live an unselfish life.

He never told of the circumstances that led to the change, but as time went on, everyone came to know and rejoice in Brainard's transformation.

III.

RECREATION.

Winning the Emblem.

"YES, we must get the Meet to-day, for that 'State Cup' looks a pile better up in Hawkeye College Library than it would any where else in the state."

"That's right, Fred, it does," replied "Spike" English, "and we don't want to be the fellows to let it go either."

The two boys were riding in the Rock-Island flyer bound for the Iowa Capitol. Two long strips of canvas outside the car, bearing in scarlet and black lettering the words "Hawkeye College Track Team," sufficiently advertised the occupants to every farm house and village as the train sped along; while the team, and the two hundred students accompanying them to the State Meet, took advantage of the one stop to throw up the windows of their coaches, and give a rousing college yell to the crowd around the low brick station.

Durnham had changed somewhat in the

year since Dumbaugh had left, but he was still the irrepressible Fred. He had not met with much success in his athletic attempts during his sophomore year; in fact some of those supercilious beings who are, themselves, too lazy to train, but are always trying to discourage a fellow unless he can beat a state record after three months' training, advised him to give it up and rest awhile. Fred took their chaffing good-naturedly, however, and kept pegging away, so that in his second season he had worked into pretty good form. "Spike" English gave him a deal of help. "Spike" was a heavy-set man, whom two years of football had pounded into as solid a specimen as any one would care to run up against, and his wind was perfect. Though Fred could keep close behind him every night in practice, he had never been able to beat him, so that the boys nicknamed him "Spike's Shadow". There was only one fault with "Spike"; he ran too "heavy", so that his ankles were apt to trouble him in the final sprint, but he had been very careful during the week before the Meet, and did not anticipate any trouble from them. In talking over the events, however, the boys agreed that "Spike" should set the pace in both the "half" and the "mile", though Fred was to stick right by him up to the finish. There was not the least rivalry between them, when they came to an intercollegiate contest; either one would work to give his mate a better chance for a place.

While they were discussing these points, Capt. Trevers came up to them. "Plotting again, I see," he said, taking a seat on the arm of the chair. "Well, that is a good sign, seven points in two events 'cinched' if Fred doesn't get run off his legs on the home stretch, and won't he feel swell with that 'II' on his sweater."

As they were nearing East Des Moines, at the very out skirts of the city, they could make out the long, low sheds of the Fair Grounds, where the afternoon games were to be held; then on a hill off to the North they got a view of the State Capitol with its gilded dome.

At the depot the team immediately packed themselves and their grips into two 'buses and hurried to the Kirkwood, impartially decorated with the colors of the half dozen competing colleges, where they proceeded to stow away a good amount of roast beef, potatoes, toast, and oranges. Ray Howell, the only fellow on the team who refused to board at the training table, called for pie as usual, and his request was met by so much raillery that he offered to bet "the pie" with every fellow on the team, that he would put the shot over thirty-six feet in the afternoon, and his bet was readily taken.

Dinner over, the boys loafed around the corridors for a while, guessing at the scores the different colleges would make, and striking up acquaintances with the men from Phillips College, who also had their headquarters at the Kirkwood; but they were glad when it came time to go to the field. As they drove out Grand Avenue and over the bridge, they passed many groups of students and alumni wearing their colors, and leaning out of the 'bus windows, the team made the street ring with the Hawkeye yells. The amphitheater presented a gay scene as they entered the grounds. Long stretches of white and blue, cardinal, purple, and scarlet and black bunting fluttered from every post and cross-piece in the grand stand.

"Now every man get around to our quarters and keep low until his event," said Coach "Mike" Stevens as the boys jumped out of the buses. The boys soon found the dressing-room under the grand stand with the scarlet "H" over the door; and most of those entered in the first events stretched themselves out at once on the cots, while "Mike" and Trevers went around to the group of officials in the judges' stand to find out who of the contestants entered were to be "protested". "Mike" was a dark-complexioned man of average height, about thirty-five years of age, but with all the vigor of his college days. He practiced medicine in Chicago, but now for the second season he had left his work in the spring, and come out to coach Hawkeye's track team for a couple of months. He had a wonderful faculty of getting the most out of a team, and had changed many a soft, awkward candidate into a strong, self-reliant athlete, so that the boys all swore by "Mike".

Just before two o'clock the first call for the
fifty-yard dash is given. "Nick" Trevers and
Harry Bartlett get into their running togs and
hurry out, for "Nick" wants to examine the
track and pick out the best places, trusting to
luck that Harry and he will draw the right
numbers. He is not disappointed in the track
either. It is in nearly as perfect condition
as one can find short of a cinder track. The
rain a few days previous had beaten it down,
while the June sun, warm, but not hot
enough to bake it, had left it as smooth and
springy as the most exacting track captain
could wish. "If the wind keeps down, there
will be some records smashed," he says to
Harry. Harry grins for answer; he is an irre-
sponsible youth, no slouch, however, when it
comes to getting over ground in short order.
He has been watching the crowd in the grand
stand, by this time packed from the top row to
the wire netting which prevents the spectators
from pushing out upon the track. And a gay
crowd it is—at least six hundred students
wearing their long streamers of college colors,
some scarcely daring to hope that their ath-

letes will carry home the silver emblem of victory, but all impatient for the contests to begin. There are some two hundred from Phillips College and about the same number from Hawkeye, while a hundred are gathered around the purple banner of Barrington University.

The State Normal School have a contingent of fifty to cheer on their athletes in the only event of which they are sure—the high jump. But the citizens far outnumber the students whose representatives are about to contend for the State Championship. Traveling men by the score, merchants, professional men, and clerks have taken an afternoon off to watch the sports. Here and there are the parents of some of the contestants, whose anxious faces show their high hopes of seeing their sons win glory for their college and themselves.

At last the men line up at the scratch and at the crack of the pistol they dash down the stretch. Hearing the report, Fred slips around the corner of the building to take a look. "The old 'Nick' first," he yells back to the boys, "and Harry a close second. Just the right way to start the thing."

The afternoon passes rapidly as the events are run off, and the points are distributed among the various colleges. Phillips College is Hawkeye's closest rival. They take first in the hammer-throw, hurdles, and pole-vault, and a generous number of seconds and thirds —those places not so eagerly fought for, but which, nevertheless, generally decide a meet. The "half" and mile run have by some mistake been placed pretty close together on the list, so after the "half" in which "Spike" and Fred come in ahead with a good lead, the management decides to make the "mile" the last event, and the boys again stretch themselves out to wait with as good grace as possible. "Nick" Trevers has chalked out on the side of the dressing-room, so that all the boys can see them, the events and the points each college gets out of them. As word from the shot-put comes in he adds: "H 1st, 36 ft. 2 in. Howell." "Just so," bursts out the Senior as he comes tearing through the door and looks at the record, "and I'm all ready for that pie too. When are you fellows going to pay your debts, eh?" "Oh shut up, you idiot," replies Trevers, "and give the boys a chance to rest," and he goes on with his figuring.

The last event but the mile run has come off and, with a troubled face, "Nick" puts down in large characters:

PHILLIPS, 36.

HAWKEYE, 36.

BARRINGTON, 22.

"There seems to be no show for us, 'Spike', " he said, going up to English who was pacing the room, "limbering up", "unless you get this 'mile'. That Phillips man, Allison, gave you fellows a hot chase in the 'half', and we can't rely on Fred in the 'mile'. A 'kid' of eighteen is sure to lose his head when it comes to a pinch, though Fred will do his best, bring us a third anyhow. Set Allison a killing pace from the start and let Fred keep up as long as he can."

The men are slipping on their "spikes" and hunting around for their "grips", as the announcer sticks his head in at the door and calls out, "Third and final call for the mile run." In a moment they are out on the track. There are only eight men to start in this race and all, except the men wearing the cardinal emblem of Phillips, are from the colleges which have not run up large enough scores to make them the cause of any anxiety. Allison draws first place and "Spike," fourth, while Fred has to content himself with last choice. They throw their sweaters to the "swipes", and take their places on the scratch, the scarlet cross at both ends of the long row of contestants. "Now keep cool, Fred, and don't lose your nerve," said "Mike" taking Fred's sweater. "Are you ready," calls the starter, "get on your marks,—set!" As the pistol snaps, the men spring forward, "Spike" jumps into the lead with his long stride, starting out at a furious pace. Allison falls in behind him, and Fred next. These three "trail" around the track, the other runners bunch and keep some yards back of the leaders from the very start.

All the contestants have left the dressing-room, and in some kind of costume or other have gathered along the side of the track to

watch the race, every one glad that his share
of the work is done. Nothing makes a track
man feel so cheerful as the consciousness of
having earned a goodly number of points for
his college; the weeks and months of training
seem short when a fellow can look back at
them as a victor; while if he has been beaten,
he still knows that the training will stand him
in good stead for another year's work.
"Nick" Trevers, Bartlett, and Howell were
standing with "Mike" at the tape, "waiting
to see 'Spike' and his shadow go flitting by,"
as Howell phrases it.

The three head men have the same order as
they pass the judges' stand, and at the tap of
the bell they settled down for the second hard
lap. "Spike" is running his usual strong
race, his legs go like clockwork, and he knows
as well as though he were holding a stop-
watch what time he is making. Three years on
the track have given him a good head for
gauging his pace. Allison is a fine specimen
of an athlete with his six feet of well knit
muscle, and it seems only a pleasure to him
to "trail" "Spike" at any pace he can set

him. "You just watch old Allison fool that
Hawkeye man on the home stretch," says a
Phillips student to his companion, "he knows
the odds at stake as well as the next man."

Fred is perhaps the best built man of the
three, trim and clean-limbed, and while not
over five feet eight, he takes a longer stride
than either of the others. He shows his lack
of experience, however, and the pace is telling
on him, so that he begins to look a little
"blowed" already, but manages to keep within
two or three yards of Allison.

There is not a word spoken in the grand
stand, every one is watching the three forms on
the other side of the field. At the quarter-
post, "Spike" seems to stop short for an instant and the Phillips man darts past him.
"What the dickens is the matter with 'Spike'!"
ejaculates Bartlett with a blank face, looking
at Trevers. "His ankles, I suppose." "Nick"
looks bluer than the boys often see him but
he has not given up hope yet; he has seen too
many races won in the last ten feet. As
"Spike" falls back, Fred quickens his pace
and the two keep together for a short distance,

Allison constantly gaining on them till he has a clear thirty yards lead. At the 220-tapes, "Spike" calls out, "Catch him, Fred, I can't go another step," and he drops out of the race. Fred pulls himself together and starts out on the fiercest sprint of his life. Only two hundred and twenty yards in which to make up thirty. He sets his teeth, clinches his fists and rushes madly down the stretch. His face seems to grow whiter at every stride, his eyes glaze, but by the sheer force of will he drives himself in the desperate pursuit. As the Phillips man half turns his head five yards from the line, he sees a pale figure with the scarlet emblem glittering on his breast. An instant and it has gained a foot on him, broken the string, and fallen to the ground.

The great crowd which had risen and watched the final struggle in oppressive silence, burst out into frantic cheers and yells. Professor Nicolls, Hawkeye's gray-haired instructor in Latin, swinging his hat in one hand and his cane in the other, rushed out of the building to where Fred lay, and helped "Mike" and "Nick" carry him around to the

dressing-rooms. Here they laid him gently
on a rubbing couch and tried to work the
aches and soreness out of his knotted and
strained muscles.

"Bless you, old man," said "Spike", limp-
ing over to the group around Fred, "but
our 'kids' are made of the right stuff. I
guess you have earned the 'H' all right, for
you lowered the State record just five seconds." "Did I, 'Spike'?" and Fred looked
up with a happy smile, "then I'm satisfied."
And so were the two hundred Hawkeye students who had watched the boy's plucky run.

"Traggles'" Suit.

"THERE'S nothing the matter with this night," remarked Dick Sleighton to a group of boys gathered at one of the down town candy stores. "Looked as if it were going to rain this afternoon, though, and I didn't make a date. Suppose she isn't at home now, so it would do no good to go up."

The boys did not seem to need an explanation of the term "she," as they asked no questions. A long silence followed. Finally a tall, athletic-looking fellow whispered to Dick, "There are the girls going down town. They look as though there was something up. Let's walk down the street and see."

Unnoticed by the group whose attention was just then turned to "swiping" peanuts, the two went out and sauntered down the street looking in all the windows. At last they stopped before a jewelry store where they seemed to be entirely absorbed in discussing some new college pins.

"Let's pretend not to see them when they come back," suggested Harry Bartlett.

"All right, here they are," returned Dick.

The last part of the remark seemed quite uncalled for, as it would have been impossible not to notice the arrival of the girls, who were giggling, of course, and loaded down with innumerable bags and bundles. They evidently had no intention of loitering, for they rushed past with a gait a professional pedestrian might have envied.

"I guess we'll have to run if we ever catch up with them," Dick remarked.

"It's too warm to exert ourselves very much. If they're in such a hurry, let's let them go," returned Bartlett, whose pride in the medal he had won last field-day in the hundred yard dash forbade him using his skill in frivolous matters.

"Oh bother, hurry up or they'll be home before we catch them, and it's after seven o'clock now, so there'll be only about half an hour anyway," growled Dick.

A block's run brought them up with the girls. "Ah, good evening. Can't we fellows be useful as well as ornamental by carrying some of your numerous bundles?"

"Why, yes, thank you, Mr. Sleighton," and Clara Nesbit heaved a sigh of relief as she piled up Dick's outstretched arms.

"Seems to me you girls always have the most packages! Why don't you put them all in one big bag? It would be ten times easier to carry."

"Oh, if they're any trouble—" began Clara.

"Oh, you know I didn't mean that. But what are all these things for, anyway? You people must be going to have a blow-out."

"Well—we were thinking of having a little feast."

"A little feast! It seems to me there is enough here for forty men."

"Worse than that, it's for four girls," retorted Clara.

They had reached the steps of Mears' Cottage and turned to watch the progress of their companions, which was not exceedingly rapid.

"Oh don't go in yet. It's fifteen minutes

at least before the bell rings," urged Dick,
notwithstanding the fact that he was beneath
a load heavy enough to draw a sympathizing
tear from the eye of an over-worked dray
horse.

"We must," answered Clara decidedly.
"We can get in now without being seen, and
if we wait fifteen minutes, we'll be sure to en-
counter some one anxiously awaiting our arrival."

"Well, I suppose we had better go then.
But I call it a shame to waste this elegant
evening," grumbled Dick. "But say, are
there any donations we could make in the
way of—well, let me see,—drinks for in-
stance?"

"Well, perhaps we might be able to use
something of the sort. It's awfully good of
you to think of it, Dick."

"What'll you have? Perhaps a little—"

"Ginger ale will do very nicely, thank you."

"At what time are these midnight revels to
be held?"

"Why, we generally consider twelve o'clock
as midnight, in this part of town."

"Indeeed, you don't mean it!"

"Well, perhaps I don't, but if you bring up your contribution at that time, we will lower the 'elevator.' Whistle down at the corner, to let us know you're coming. And be sure not to make a noise when you get up here."

"All right, it's a go, and I guess that's all that is left for us, too."

"If you intended that for a pun, my opinion is, the sooner you go the better."

"Oh, I beg your pardon. I didn't intend that for a pun—but we'll go. Well, then, till 'the iron tongue of midnight doth tell twelve.' So, ladies and gentlemen, thanking you one and all for your kind attention and liberal patronage we shall now close with the last act of 'Exit.' So 'au revoir, but not good-bye.'"

"Good-bye, many thanks for carrying these small bundles."

"Don't mention it, the pleasure was all mine."

"Well, I'm glad you liked it."

"I certainly did. It isn't a bad thing now

and then for a fellow to put his athletic training to some good use."

"That's right. By the way there are several
loose boards in this walk—"

"Really I think we had better go. Good
night, ladies. You have one and three-quar-
ters seconds to get in the house before the bell
rings."

This time the boys were actually off.

"Pretty nice girl, that Miss Holmes, don't
you think so?" asked Bartlett.

"Oh, I don't know. Why yes, of course I
think she's all right," replied Dick, coming
out of a reverie. "But didn't it strike
you that Clara was provoked about something?"

"I didn't notice it. She'll get over it if
she is," was Jack's ready consolation. "But
say, that new suit you have on is pretty
smooth."

"Do you think so? I rather like it myself.
But I've got to go down town now. I'll turn
into the 'Den' and study after a while if I
can't find anything better to do."

The girls in the meantime had entered the

house, escaping the ever watchful eye of the
matron, and had gone to their room.

"Where shall I put all these things?" asked
Winnifred Holmes. She had been there only
a few days on a visit to her cousin, and so
had not been thoroughly initiated into all the
mysteries of college life.

"Oh, throw your bundles back of that door.
Nobody will ever see them. Be careful or
that screen will tumble down again. It
ought to go to 'gym' and learn to stand up
straight. Oh dear, there's this Greek lesson
to get and a 'psych' lesson too. Will you ex-
cuse me, my dear, if I proceed to study? I
positively must not flunk to-morrow, for I dis-
graced myself in every recitation to-day. I
piled up a lot of books and magazines on that
table for you, if you want to read; and if you
prefer to talk to someone, Nell said she would
like to have you come in and see her; she's 'Conservatory' and doesn't have to study at night."

"Oh, don't bother about me, I'll amuse myself all right."

"Mail!" rang out a voice from the upper
part of the corridor.

"Any for me?" shouted Clara, rushing to the door.

"A paper is all."

"Seems to me that I might get a letter once in a while. Newspapers are so very consoling," grumbled Clara.

"Well, to return to that 'long-suffering divine Odysseus.' Just imagine the trouble we would have been spared, if Paris had only assisted him out of this world before those awful wanderings began."

"Look at your lamp. It's going out!"

"Oh, it hasn't been filled to-day. Now we'll have to blow it out and go on the balcony to fill it. You know it's against rules to fill it inside the house after dark."

After this was done, quiet reigned for a time. Then came a rap on the door, and without waiting for an answer, a girl dashed in, grabbed a book from a shelf, exclaiming as she left the room, "May I borrow your Latin 'dic'?"

"Oh, Win, please put a 'busy' sign on the door or I won't be able to get a lesson to-night," sighed Clara. When the half-past nine bell rang, she was still studying, but at ten, she threw aside her books, announcing that the last part of her psychology would have to be left until chapel time next morning.

"Hadn't we better put out the light for a while at least?" suggested Winifred.

"Oh, no, we'll put a shawl over the transom so the light won't shine through."

"Would you be suspended if they caught us?"

"I expect so," answered Clara, making a good show of recklessness.

"Let's not do it then."

"Oh, I'm not afraid. There's no need of any one's knowing it, if we're only careful. But we must not forget to wake Bess and Lil about half-past eleven. They'll never forgive us if we don't. Suppose we make the fudges now, so they'll have time to cool. We can't pop the corn until everybody is asleep, or they'd smell it. The Welsh rare-bit will have to wait until the girls bring in their chafing-dish."

"Do you pop the corn on that little oil-stove?"

"Oh, gracious no. It would take all next week to pop it that way. We always use the lamp to pop corn with. But be quiet, for methinks I hear foot-steps approaching on horseback down the corridor of time."

The sound of the steps came nearer and then died away in the distance. For the first time complete silence fell on everything. One by one the lights down the hall disappeared. Soon a mouse starting out on an exploring expedition caused the girls' hearts to beat anxiously. Winnifred was seized with a panic.

"Oh, I know there is some one in the hall by that door—I hear the breathing."

"Nonsense," said Clara. " ' 'Tis but the wind, or the car rattling o'er the—' "

"No, I tell you there is some one there. You must not go into the hall to get those girls. Just think how terribly your father and mother would feel if you were suspended. I'm going to lock the door and keep the key. There now, you can't get out of the room."

"You'll have to stand the consequences then, to-morrow. They will be so mad that probably they won't speak to us at all."

"Oh, I don't care, if only we aren't caught."

"There's Dick whistling now."

"Let down the 'elevator,'" came Dick's whisper loud enough to drown ordinary conversation.

"Here it is. Be careful and don't talk so loud, Dick, please."

"All right, now steady."

The girls pulled it up. Just as they took the bottles out, an idea came to them.

"Oh, we haven't any corkscrew."

"Here's one, I'll throw it up."

"Oh, don't. I'll be afraid to open it anyway, because it pops so. What can we do? We'll have to let them down again and let you open them."

"Yes, and a lot would be left in the bottle by the time you got it up there again. I'll tell you what—I'll climb to the edge of the porch and you can hand a bottle to me."

"All right. Be careful and don't get on those nails we put up there for the decorations, field-day."

"I'll look out. Here I am. Now, can you

reach a bottle out the window?"

"Here it is."

Dick put the corkscrew in and pulled.

"Young ladies, what does this mean?"

The door had opened, and when the shawl hanging from the transom had been pushed aside, the figure of the matron was revealed. There was a report from the window as though a pistol had been fired, a scrambling, a sound of something tearing, the thud of a heavy body falling on the ground.

Winnifred began to weep. Clara was irresolute, whether to face the battle with the matron, or rush to the window to see if Dick were hurt. At last, being reassured by the sound of life below, she turned to greet the enemy.

"There is no need of saying anything, Miss Nesbit. I think I understand the situation perfectly. You will immediately close your window, and put out your light, and in the morning I should like to see you. Next time I would advise you to be sure the door is locked," and turning, Miss Dorcas left the room.

"You didn't turn the lock all the way!" ex-claimed Clara. "Oh Winnifred, do you think Dick is hurt badly?"

.   .   .   .

A week later Dick was going to the post-office with one of the boys, when suddenly his friend asked:

"Say, old fellow, are you and Miss Nesbit going to play quits? You haven't been up there for a whole week."

"Oh, I don't know. Been studying pretty hard for a while. Haven't had much time to fool away."

"I didn't know you called that fooling away your time. But here comes ' Traggles'," went on Bartlett. The individual in question was a simple old colored man, a great favorite with the boys, upon whom they bestowed many of their cast-off garments, besides a great deal of attention.

"He's got a new coat, too. My, but it's swell for the old fellow. Nearly comes up to your new suit, Dick, and I bet the next cent I get, that the material is almost like yours.

Let's stop him and find out where he got so much 'swelldom'."

The old man came up. He looked odd enough in a light spring coat of the latest cut. The only peculiar thing about the coat was a three-cornered tear on one of the sleeves, and some dark spots scattered over it quite generally.

"Oh, I'm in a terrible hurry. I can't stop," exclaimed Dick, suddenly awakening to the fact.

"Come to think about it, Dick, why don't you wear your new suit? I haven't seen it since the first time you wore it."

"I dunno,—but when I came to examine it by daylight, I found the color was hideous, and besides it didn't fit at all," answered Dick, looking thoughtfully at the clouds reddened by the setting sun.

Coach "Chubby".

BARRINGTON UNIVERSITY and Hawkeye College were fighting out to an un-
certain finish their annual contest on the
gridironed field.

The excitement was of a sort engendered
by a rivalry dating back to the memorable
year when "Dad" Bryon, Princeton's famous
end of 188—, introduced the first Hawkeye
eleven to foot-ball and incidentally to the
players of Barrington University. Although
acting the part of host on that occasion,
Bryon's proteges sent their friendly antago-
nists home with nothing to their credit beyond
consoling thoughts of what might have been.
The Hawkeye players had amassed twenty-four
points, to be recorded as the score of their
first foot-ball victory.

Year after year had worn away, and the
meeting of the Barrington and Hawkeye teams
had developed into an event of paramount

athletic interest to the two schools thus repre-
sented. Then it was that old "grads" sought
to reassemble; to slap each other on the back
and recall past days; dilating on the degen-
eracy of the present, notably from the sports-
man's point of view. On this particular occasion they were much in evidence. There were
Tom Hurley and "Fussy" Williams, ex-cap-
tains of Barrington and Hawkeye respectively,
squabbling over the game with the same ardor
displayed a few years before when they were
pitted against each other in gubernatorial
capacity. The lively conversation between
these two veterans was a feature that attracted no little attention in their immediate
vicinity. A prominent figure in the crush of
spectators was a tall, gray-bearded old gentleman. It was soon whispered about that he
was one of the Hawkeye trustees, who had come
a hundred miles to see what the game was
like, in order to determine whether he really
approved of it. He had preconceived notions
of a brutal warfare in which broken noses
and twisted limbs were painfully frequent.

To the younger generation, the reminiscent remarks overheard here and there, suggested pleasantly the wreath of tradition that was beginning to crown their cherished field, the scene of many a well-earned victory.

The game was drawing to a close. The besweatered "subs" along the lines were following with closest scrutiny every move that changed the position of the ball, and emitting laconic grunts of approval or censure, as the play pleased or disappointed them. No longer did the Hawkeye mascot proudly wag his ribboned tail before an admiring assemblage, but true to his canine instinct, he was pursuing the sprightly chipmunk, leaving the outcome of the game in the hands of the Fates, and twenty-two stalwart young giants.

· The gruff little linesman who kept the time had grudgingly volunteered the information that nine minutes were left to play. As yet no score had requited the lively encouragement from the rival factions. As the remaining time became steadily less, the excitement increased proportionately.

Two precious minutes had slipped by, during which the ball changed hands a few times

with little result. Then came a grand opportunity for an attempt to kick a goal from
the field. Hawkeye shoved the ball to the
'Varsity's fifteen-yard line, but not the most
desperate efforts of King, Hawkeye's dashing
half-back, could pass that point. Twice they
had advanced very near to the last white-
washed line, that meant victory, and twice
had four downs caused a groan of disappointment from the Hawkeye contingent, which
was pressing heavily, with fevered agitation
against the ropes on the west side of the
grounds. A confident and lusty cheer arose
opposite them where the Barrington following, scarcely so numerous, yet equally vocif-
erous, had taken up its position.

"Is Jack dead crazy?" was the surprising
interrogation to which "Chubby" Grant gave
utterance. "Chubby" was a tousled and
dumpy specimen of humanity, attired in a
unique athletic garb, half foot-ball, semi-
base-ball in make-up. This was the boy's
first year at Hawkeye. No one could state
positively where his home was. Undeniable,
however, were the facts of his classification as

" Is Jack dead crazy ? "

a Prep and his invariable attendance at
the daily practice. One afternoon he had
been nearly beside himself with joy when the
captain had allowed him to play a couple of
minutes on the scrub, while Jones was lacing
up his jacket. The boys admired his plucky
spirit, and he was always granted the privilege
of holding their sweaters. With an important, business-like air, he would   help in
stretching them on after the first half, and in
stripping them off after the fray recom-
menced.

By virtue of his official prerogative,
"Chubby" could view the game inside the
ropes, which were creaking from the spas-
modic pushes of the mass of eager spectators.
He watched keenly every move out on the
field and noting the mistake in not trying for a
goal, he had blurted out his, as yet, unanswered
question.

"Sit down, my lad, sit down! How d'ye expect one to see the game, with you standing
in the way?"

It was the gray-bearded trustee. In his
mind the problem was solved and he was a

strong convert to foot-ball. About twenty
minutes before, he had left his seat in the
stand, and was elbowing his way excitedly
through one of the densest yelling-squads, that
he might come closer to the scene of action.
He was as enthusiastic as a Freshman, and as
exacting. "Chubby" minded him not; the
trustee was not "in it" just then. It was a
critical time. Thompson, the big center, was
just about to snap the ball to the Hawkeye
quarter on Barrington's fifteen-yard line. A
slight lull ensued, so that a single voice was
audible at some distance.

The players are near at hand and their heavy
breathing is painfully distinct. The Hawkeye right tackle stops the game full forty
seconds to regulate a refractory shin-guard.

"Take out that time there, you linesman," shout several imperious voices. One
of the "subs" avails himself of the opportunity, to tighten the bandage on the little
half-back's head. All is ready again. The
lines crouch into position and play is resumed
after a tantalizing delay. The signal com-
mences but is interrupted by a determined

protest from the side. "Why in thunder don't you let 'Buck' kick a goal from the field?"

The captain glanced sternly in the direction of the sound, relaxing his severity somewhat as he perceived it was only "Chubby." Then followed the signal for a line plunge.

The umpire, however, continually on the alert, thought he detected some side-line coaching, and shaking a warning finger at the sturdy little "sub", threatened to have him put off the field.

With this play, Hawkeye's second opportunity had slipped by. The ball was now in Barrington's possession ready for an advance out of danger, while a stirring shout of relief volleyed forth from the University element.

Captain Lyman compressed his lips a little more firmly and implored the men with "Smash 'em! Tear up that interference, Armstrong! Play your game, Cub! Now—." All his entreaties could not prevent a steady retrogression centerwards, and a consequent feeling of discouragement took possession of the anxious wearers of the scarlet and black. The purple of Barrington flaunted madly from cane and parasol, for their champions seemed at last to have struck a winning gait.

Several stop-watches have registered two minutes left to play. Just now a mighty roar shakes the atmosphere. "Hawkeye's ball!" is the hoarse shout passed down the lines. Pandemonium has broken loose. Only twenty-five yards; then, victory! Can they struggle across that intervening strip?

On the first down, King, the fleet half, is started around the end. Smoothly the interference precedes the runner in perfect formation. Surely they will gain this time. Not so thinks the University right end and he hurls every ounce of his scant hundred and forty pounds into the oncoming rush. Down they go, one, two, three, and quick as a flash the tackle is through the opening and brings the half to earth with more force than grace. "Second down and six yards to gain," shouts the referee.

Once more a line play is tried. Where a clean hole should have been, the stocky guard of the University was ready to embrace the nimble runner, which he accomplished so handily as to cause a loss of two feet of stubbornly contested sod. Again a crisis has come, and the grounds are as quiet as a churchyard.

Some one was seen to run out a few yards on the field. Waving his arms as well as two extra sweaters and a red blanket permitted, he roared: "Lyman, you've got to win the game! Try that goal and you can do it easy!"

It was the irrepressible "sub" once more, and this time he paid for his temerity by being courteously, yet firmly, escorted outside the ropes and beyond the fence, at the umpire's request, while the crowd looked on and laughed. The remedy was rather more heroic than Mr. Spalding's rule-book warrants, but the offense was of extreme gravity; at least, so reasoned the umpire. However, "Chubby's" mission was accomplished. "8-12-6-7-28," gasped Captain Lyman, and "Buck" Miller ran backwards five yards, eagerly awaiting the pass. Then came the "gamiest" fight of the day. Nobly did the Barrington forwards struggle to get through and block that kick. Their right half-back, the mighty Harrison, leaped recklessly over the line, in hope of reach-

ing the full-back in time; but the Hawkeye
quarter was on his mettle and catching his
opponent in the air, threw him heavily. Each
man did his best. So effective was the defence
that "Buck" was undisturbed. From out
that mass of tugging, steaming humanity, the
leathern spheroid shot serenely forth, and
speeding on its way fell directly above the
cross-bar of the goal—and five points were
scored to the credit of Hawkeye.

It was all over, save the maddened delight
of five hundred college students whose defend-
ers had won a tremendous victory. The
people swarmed out on the field in good-natured confusion. The reverend trustee forgot
his dignity, and, in amiable frame of mind, patted the players on the back and congratulated
them for their success, in true undergraduate
fashion. The game had been too close for
enjoyment, and now that it was really saved,
joy passed all restraint.

Not a man of the eleven walked from the
field that day. The earth seemed far too base
for such heroes to tread.

Shoulders there were in plenty to furnish

cushions for the athletes' quivering, aching muscles.

The more modest tried to elude this enforced march of triumph, but the happy mob soon spied each man and hoisted him, resisting, to a higher "coign of vantage". The captain had disappeared almost as quickly as the Barrington delegation. On all sides loud calls of "Lyman, Lyman, we want Lyman!" resounded. Then the crowd began to converge at the gates. A Barrington straggler would come along occasionally, and was at once singled out for general mild abuse.

The gay procession of enthroned athletes was pushing its way out. As the gate was reached, Lyman greeted his comrades, carrying on his brawny shoulders the chunky little "sub" who had virtually won the day.

"We head this march, don't we, 'Chubby'?" "Chubby" gave an affirmative grunt, and then, as a realization came home to every one that the game had really been saved by that last brilliant play, which the little fellow had forfeited his own pleasure to bring to pass, cheers for the gallant "Chub" well nigh overcame that worthy, and he squirmed in vain to escape what he considered indecorous popularity.

Five years later, "Chubby" was captain of that Hawkeye eleven which never met defeat. The dearest relic in ex-Captain Grant's room is an old foot-ball, suspended amongst his photographs over the mantel-piece and bearing on its surface the roughly painted, mystical characters, 5-0.

IV.

IN SERIOUS VEIN.

Back in the Sixties.

THE large south-east room of the Old Hall was in more confusion than usual this morning. Good Mrs. Bonebright had come to "straighten up a bit," but had been ordered out, "until later, Mrs. Bonebright;" and she had departed wondering.

The early morning sun looked in the east windows on an unusual spectacle. This was unquestionably the best room of the house in which to loaf, and it was seldom used for any other purpose. The window-seat was wide, and adorned with a few substantial cushions, presents from girl friends, or "swiped," when making calls. And one of the surprising things was, that this morning there was no one lounging there. The book-shelves were filled with good, substantial, clean-looking text-books, except one shelf where the volumes of Field, Stevenson, college yarns and novels were well worn. But the sign, "Rare volumes sel-

(163)

dom if ever handled," which belonged over the shelves, lay with several others of the same kind in the ashes of the fire-place.

The table, for once, seemed to be a study table; books and papers were piled so high that a young man seated at the farther end was scarcely visible. He was busy glancing over a pile of papers, taking up one and at the same time throwing down another, running his hands through his curly black hair and grumbling something in an undertone about this "confounded grind," while his dark blue eyes wore a troubled expression. He was evidently intent upon what he was doing, although not with an air of thoroughly enjoying his present situation.

Yes, this was Jack Harrington. He had just opened Bryce's "American Commonwealth," and was taking notes, when a loud knock was heard at the door, and not waiting for a response, Ned Burton rushed into the room, saying as he met Jack's angry glance:

"What, not going to Chapel, old man?"

"No, hang it, not going anywhere," replied Jack, in a manner not inviting further counsel.

"Well, I'll be dubbed, what in thunder ails you? No suicidal intentions, I hope; looks as if you might be making out your will," said Ned, picking up one of the numerous papers scattered over the table.

"If you had half an eye, I should think you could see. This blamed paper for political science was due a month ago, and Hicks has jerked me up regularly after every recitation, and said if I did not have it to-morrow he'd ——"

"O the deuce, Jack, if that's all that ails you, come along, old man. This is Decoration Day, and Prof. Mitchell always makes his customary address, and really, you want to see how the girls have decorated the slabs containing the names of our heroic dead. There goes the last bell. Come along, Jack; let old Hicks wait another day. He needs to cultivate patience," said Ned, as he turned towards the door.

Jack muttered something to the effect that he wished to be left alone, and Ned hurried down the stairs, wondering what had come over his chum.

"I never knew anything to trouble that fellow before, much less a 'pol sci' paper, but stranger things have happened," said Ned to himself, as he entered the Chapel.

Ned might better have understood Jack's unusual manner, had he known that, while at breakfast that morning, Jack had received a telegram from his father, to the effect that he was on his way home from Denver and would spend the night with him.

Now Jack was one of those jolly good fellows, whom all the boys liked and who thought it far better to get "D" in his work and be "in the push," as he called it, than to bother over Weber's Law, much less Horace. He would leave that nonsense to the girls.

But the arrival of the telegram had, for a time, put all these notions out of his head. Jack's father was a graduate of Hawkeye in '67, and felt a deep interest in the work of his son. So Jack was now straining every nerve to be able to give his paper before the class on the following day, and convince his father of the genuine hard work he was doing, while at the same time he might be more sure of the "fifty" he wanted at once. So the morning wore away and afternoon passed into evening. Jack was just hurrying down the steps of the Old Hall, when he was hailed by, "Well, old boy, where now? Are you really awake to the fact that there is a world outside that den of yours?—To the '6:40'?" as Jack turned in the direction of the station. "What's up now—Mamma coming?"

"No," said Jack, "Father is on his way home from Denver and telegraphed he would spend the night with me."

"Well, you needn't have wasted your time trying to bluff me about that 'pol sci' article. It didn't go down a little bit, but really, old man, it's a wonder to me you have common sense enough left after a day of *real* hard work to know where you are at," said Ned.

"See here, old fellow," said Jack, turning quickly upon him, "let me give you a pointer. You're not to mention this day's work, and, in fact, my work is not to be mentioned in his presence, as you value your life, old man, not a syllable."

"I always thought I was a friend of yours—but how long will he stay?"

"Goes on to-morrow night's limited to Davenport," said Jack.

This short conversation was interrupted by the whistle of the approaching train, just as the boys reached the depot platform. A minute later Jack was doing all the honors of an obedient son. "Father, let me introduce my friend, Mr. Burton."

"Mr. Harrington, I'm glad to meet you," said Ned, offering his hand.

Mr. Harrington looked steadily into his face for a moment, and then said, in a voice showing not a little interest: "Can it be possible that you're the son of John Burton, '67?"

"I have the honor, I believe."

"Well! well! John was one of my very best friends during the sixties, and friends were friends in those days, the darkest days this country has ever known. Life at old Hawkeye was very different then, from what it is now, I imagine." By this time they had reached the street leading to Ned's boarding-hall, and after a few words at the corner

Ned, with a tip of his cap and a "good-bye," was gone.

"Come over to the room after supper, Ned, and father will tell us some more about the life of old Hawkeye in his days."

"It's a go," called back Ned.

"That's the queerest specimen of humanity in this college," said Jack, as he and his father turned down High Street, "forever harping on war. He'd be just in his element if he could marshal the company out on dress parade, but he'd be the one to leave at the first smell of powder, you can bet on that."

"You can't always tell, Jack. There's nothing like war to bring out what's in a man. His father was one of the best and bravest soldiers I ever knew—always ready and at his post for duty."

Mr. Harrington seemed for the while to be living over again the scenes of thirty years ago and did not notice that they were already nearing the Old Hall.

The south-east room at eight o'clock contrasted greatly with the same room as we saw it in the morning. The table was neat, with just the right number of books lying carelessly on one side to give the impression of student life. Although it was the thirtieth of May, a bright fire burned in the grate—the unseemly signs were gone, and the college pictures on the mantel and in the tennis net were dusted and neatly arranged.

Jack was pleased with Mrs. Bonebright's work.

Mr. Harrington was examining the foot-ball which hung above the couch in one corner, and listening to Jack's story of the victory in which it figured, when the usual crowd of boys dropped in, holding an animated discussion over the morning's chapel talk. They were somewhat surprised and silenced as they in turn made the acquaintance of Jack's father. But this lasted only a moment, for they had loafed in comfort so often in the old south room that they could have faced a faculty meeting there with composure.

"Sit down, fellows, anywhere; make yourselves comfortable," said Jack.

"Well, this is solid comfort," said Dick Sleighton, as he threw himself on the rug in front of the open fire. "But where's Ned? This must be his 'psych' evening."

"Did you ever know him to stay away for that?" remarked Downley, otherwise known as "Duke," seating himself in a comfortable chair. Just at this moment the door opened, and in walked Ned, somewhat out of breath.

"Hello, fellows. Good evening, Mr. Harrington," said Ned, as he threw off his light overcoat and stepped toward the fire. "Mr. Harrington, you're going to tell us something of old Hawkeye in the early sixties; the boys want to hear it, too—don't you boys?"

"Ned's everlasting theme again," whispered Dick to his next neighbor. "I wish to goodness we could give that idiot a taste of bloodshed."

Mr. Harrington crossed the room and took the chair which Jack had placed for him in front of the fireplace. He looked with kindly interest into the faces of the boys gathered about him. "Well, my young friends," he began,—"this is such a contrast to the early sixties that I can hardly believe it is the same old Hawkeye. The little college had been dedicated but a short time before, and it stood almost alone on the prairie. It seems wonderful what development has been made in the last thirty years."

"Your father, Mr. Burton, and I used to room in a small white house some distance east of the college building. We had one little room not much bigger than a dry goods box. It was very different from this, I can assure you. It had a bed and a stove in it, and we had to measure our movements carefully before we made them. Burton was always threatening to pick the stove up and set it out in the hall. When he enlisted, he said: 'Well, that stove won't trouble me for a while.' He always liked to joke and we used to have some great times. I missed him more than any of the other fellows, I think, for we were constantly together. He was the leading spirit among all the boys. We knew, too, just what a struggle he had undergone when he made up his mind to enlist. Why, that fellow walked four days and swam two streams in order to come here. He knew how to appreciate what he was getting. But he had a high sense of duty, and when he made up his mind as to what was right, nothing could stop him. He enlisted on the second of December and was sent straight to the front. The boys used to come up to the room almost every evening to know if I had heard any news from Burton. After the battle of Philippi he was made captain of his company. From that time on, I heard no word from him for weeks. College life was unbroken in its routine of study, except when news came from the front. Then we used to go into the small, narrow recitation rooms of the one college building, day after day, with no thought of what we should have prepared, but wholly absorbed in the newspaper reports of the last engagement."

"Didn't you get 'E's'?" interrupted Jack.

"War isn't essential for that condition of affairs, at least not now," said Dick in an undertone.

"Oh, the faculty forgave us much in those days; they were as interested as we were. The question uppermost in the hearts of many of us was whether to enlist or not. Soon after the beginning of the new year, Davis and Saw-

yer, both Juniors, decided to go. Poor Davis!
He had a drooping lid and tried three times
before he was mustered in. The last time,
bound to go, in some unaccountable way he
turned his head from the examiner so that his
eye escaped detection. But his career was
short. He was killed at Fort Donelson.
Just as the news of his death reached us, ten
of us boys were on the point of enlisting, and
instead of weakening our resolve, it only made
us more determined to cast aside our Homers
for the sterner discipline of Hardy's tactics.
It's no use trying to tell you boys how hard it
was for us to go and leave those who for many
reasons could not. Our little college was almost broken up, so small was the number left.

"We were mustered in down on the river
at Davenport, and were placed in a company about to be sent south. Just before leaving, I received a letter from Burton. He
was in Tennessee, and the anticipation of
possibly seeing him, compensated in part for
the hardships we had to undergo. For, after
a painful experience of marching through
mud and water, cold and snow, with some-

times not even hard-tack and coffee, we didn't
see the pleasure of war in exactly the same
light as we had a few months previous.

"One of our boys, Joe Smith, created a good
deal of fun for the company. When we
were being mustered in, Joe laughingly gave as
his reason for enlisting, that he wished to see
the sights. So when even hard-tack was lacking, and there was no place to sleep, save the
frozen ground with not even a blanket, we
would comfort Joe by telling him he was 'seeing the sights.' Just before the battle of Shiloh, we were encamped several miles from the
city, when the order came to be ready to move
at any moment. We had been marching all
these weeks and now, for the first time, there
was a chance to go to the front.

"Poor Joe! When he heard the orders, a
deathly pallor came over his face and he said,
'I can't go, Captain, I'm sick.' Captain
Jones drew himself up to his full height and
said: 'You've heard my orders, Mr. Smith.'
'But Captain, I'm sick.' 'You'll march with
your company, sir!' I never saw a fellow so
frightened. We guyed him a bit, and told

him he'd probably see some more 'sights,' and there was nothing for him to do but go. The orders came and, half an hour later, we arrived on the field of battle and were ordered to storm a hill which the Confederates were holding. It was a terrible position, but we marched across the open field, directly in range of the enemy's cannon, men falling on all sides; just as we were climbing the last rampart, poor Joe was all but over, when the eye of an escaping 'Johnnie' saw him. He fired, and Joe fell. During the terrible night that followed, Joe's face was missed, and when 'Doc' Wilmot called the roll in the morning, there was no 'here' in answer to his name. We felt sure he had not deserted. He never would have done that, in spite of his fear, and besides, he was with us when we made the turn. We knew he was killed, and some of us wanted to go in search of the body, that we might take word of his last resting place to his mother, if we should get through alive. But our orders were to move forward. With heavy hearts we took up our line of march, having sent word back to Herndon that we had left

Joe's poor body on the field of Shiloh. That was to me one of the hardest things of the whole war, to leave a friend dead on the field.

"A long time afterwards, one afternoon while encamped with Grant's army before Vicksburg, we had the good fortune to run across Burton. I tell you it was like meeting one's own brother. We received that day fresh letters from the North. What comfort and cheer they brought to us! Letters from college, containing longed-for news from old Hawkeye. Every word was more welcome than a good beefsteak would have been, and that's saying a good deal, for we were then on pretty short rations. Burton being with us that night, we all sat around the camp-fire and talked of our college days. We talked over all the boys who had enlisted, and we could recall but two who were dead—Davis and Joe. At the mention of Joe's death, Burton jumped up, exclaiming:

'Joe! Why, boys, he's in Libby Prison; was taken there along with many other prisoners after the battle of Shiloh. I saw a record of it in a Richmond paper.'

"We could not believe it till Burton had gone to his tent and produced the paper. Yes, Joe was alive, but that was all. Libby was next thing to death. I confess I always thought that, between being taken there as prisoner and being shot, I should prefer the latter. Well, after this excitement had somewhat cooled down, we talked over everything that had taken place before or since we left college, for Burton must know everything. At last he proposed that we should sing to old Hawkeye, and we sang college songs till Clemens and I were ordered out on picket duty. The night was still and cold, with a bright moon. Every sound could be distinctly heard. Along about two in the morning I heard Clemens call out, 'Who goes there?' I was by his side in a moment and we leveled our guns as we saw a figure step out from the shadows of the trees. There was a man, gaunt and worn, with scarcely any clothing. He almost staggered forward, and, raising his hands as a sign of surrender, said: 'Don't fire, boys, for the sake of old Hawkeye, don't!' In spite of his dreadful appearance, at the sound of that word, it

flashed over me that that might be Joe;
thoughtlessly, I dropped my gun and ran
forward, just in time to catch him as he fell
from sheer exhaustion. It was Joe. He had
indeed escaped in some mysterious way and
had made perilous search for his old comrades,
finally succeeding in reaching Grant's forces.
The dying notes of our college songs had guid-
ed him straight to our picket line."

Mr. Harrington sat for a few moments silent,
looking into the fire. The boys said nothing.
Then he looked around with a smile and
added, "So you see after all, Joe had more experience and saw more 'sights' than the rest
of us."

For the Scarlet and Black.

GEORGE LAWRENCE sat alone in his room studying. It was a miserably rainy night, and he thanked his lucky stars half a dozen times that the senior girl whom he was to have escorted to the Alpha Nu reception had been suddenly called home to attend the wedding of a relative. He was sick and tired of receptions, anyway, and as for the girls— well, of course there was *one* away off in a little Ohio village who received regularly a square envelope, addressed in a very masculine hand, and having the Herndon postmark distinctly visible in the upper right-hand corner—but for girls in general he didn't care a snap of his finger, and to-night he smiled complacently to himself every few minutes as he heard the old town hacks splashing through the mud in the direction of College Hill.

He was studying, though he hardly knew why, for Friday nights were usually occupied in having "times" with the boys and all preparation for Monday's recitations was squeezed into a couple of hours on Saturday. But to-night all the others in the hall had deserted their rooms, and he realized that it was a golden opportunity to brush up a little on psychology. He dug away for about half an hour. Herbart's theories were troublesome, to say the least, and he found that he was nodding in spite of himself, when a resounding whack on the door caused him to jump up with a start.

"Come in," he called, throwing Herbart into the nearest corner. The door opened with a bang and in burst Ned Albright, closely followed by a man some dozen years his senior, whose build and proportions at once suggested the athlete, while his dress and manner as clearly distinguished him as a business man.

"Hello, old man! Not studying, are you?"

"Hello, Ned! Well, not so you'd notice it. Just pounding away a little on this old 'psych'," replied George, glancing in the direction of the stranger.

"Sorry for you from the top of my head upwards," went on the rollicking Ned. "O, Lawrence, my friend, Mr. Stanley. Stanley is an old chum of my brother's. They were class-mates, you know. Graduated along about '87. Friend of the family too, you know. Just going through the burg on his way south and stopped off to see me for an hour or so. He used to inhabit this den of yours in the old days and wanted to run up and see how things looked."

"Glad to meet you, Mr. Stanley. Shake to the honor of the old room," and Lawrence extended his hand in such genuine comradeship, that the visitor felt at home at once.

"It's the same old place," he said, glancing about the room. "Put the study table in that corner, the cane rack in this, and half a dozen more photos on the mantel, and I wouldn't believe that ten years had passed since I last crammed Greek in that old study chair. O, those were great old times," he continued. "I would give five years out of my business experience just to have my senior year back again."

"Well, you were a big man in your day, and

you know that makes all the difference in the world," said Ned, who had been six months a Senior and took no small amount of pride in the fact. "Yes, I rather like being a Senior myself."

"Don't doubt it a bit," put in George, "but get a move on yourself and shove that chair in front of the fire-place while I undermine this pyramid of gent's furnishing goods. If we keep your friend standing in the corner much longer, I wouldn't give my last year's tennis racket for what he thinks of our hospitality."

"Why, man, you're getting most awfully fastidious all of a sudden. Usually any old thing is good enough to sit on in this vicinity."

"O, don't trouble yourself, Mr. Lawrence; it won't be the first time I have stood up in this room for want of a place to sit down," and Stanley continued contemplating the picture over the mantel-piece.

Lawrence, however, soon restored things to order by piling everything into a great heap on the bed. Then he wheeled a couple of chairs in front of the fire which Ned had set to blazing by throwing among the embers a couple of copies of *Scarlet and Black*.

"Is that a picture of your '97 Glee Club?" asked Stanley, after they had made themselves comfortable.

"Which one?" inquired Ned. "George is such a Glee Club fiend he has tacked up all the Glee Club pictures since he was a Prep."

"The one in the middle with the ribbon around it," and Stanley designated the one in question with a vigorous flourish of his cane.

"Yes," answered Lawrence, "that's the latest. And it's an all right crowd, if I do say it myself. We are off for our annual tour week after next, you know, and we expect to take things by storm. We haven't put in six months of hard work for nothing."

"Good for the Glee Club! I see the old-time spirit still lives—but who is the little fellow in the left-hand corner, with the large eyes and curly hair?"

"O, that's Brooks—Jim Brooks, or Jimmy, as we call him. A Freshman this year and a capital fellow, if he does look like a girl. And such a voice —too high and bird-like for

a tenor, but with more real music in it than
any soprano you could rake up in seventeen
states. Ever since he's been here the whole
town has been wild over him, and the Director
of the School of Music says he hasn't had
such a voice in years."

"He's a comical little duffer, too," put in
Ned. "No one's ever glum when Jimmy's
around. He knocks a fit of the blues so hard
that things seem green by contrast," and the
Senior gravely caressed his mustache. "Yes,
I don't know what we'd do without him," went
on Lawrence. "We have no end of fun with
the little fellow. He's as sly as a mouse but
he can't keep out of scrapes, and the fellows
have got so they play all kinds of jokes on
him. I sometimes think we're a pretty poor
lot, but then he's so good-natured you couldn't
make him mad if you tried a week." And Lawrence complacently balanced himself on the
back legs of his chair.

No one seemed inclined to continue the conversation and Ned seized the opportunity of
casting several admiring glances at himself in
the mirror opposite. Stanley sat with his eyes

still fixed upon the picture. Suddenly he
looked around and said quietly but earnestly,
"How old is he?"

There was something in his voice which
caused Ned to look very sober for a moment,
and Lawrence so far forgot himself as to lose
his balance and bump his head with a whack
against the wall.

"Why, er—seventeen I guess. One of the
boys said he'd be eighteen next Easter," and
Lawrence rubbed the bruised spot vigorously.

Stanley's cane rattled unheeded on the hearth.
He leaned his head on his hands and gazed in-
tently at the glowing coals. Finally he looked
up, and it was not without a touch of sadness in
his tone that he said slowly, "Well, that's
queer!"

"What's the matter?" demanded the others
in one breath.

Stanley took out his watch and glanced first
at it, then at Ned. "We've got just three-
quarters of an hour before that train comes,"
he said. "If you want to spare the time, I'll
try to explain. Maybe you wouldn't mind
hearing the whole thing."

"Let's have it by all means," assented Ned, and Lawrence flung himself on the floor before the fire with, "Psychology be hanged!" Stanley crossed one leg over the other and leaned back in his chair.

"Well," said he, "you fellows may think me superstitious, or foolish or any thing you've a mind to call it, but what you have been telling me about that Jim Brooks of yours is a puzzler. When I was a Senior here, a little Freshman entered college. That was nothing unusual, only this was a particular Freshman. He was just seventeen, had light blue eyes and curly hair and was as handsome a youngster as I ever set eyes upon. His name was David Clark. Everybody liked him from the first. I verily believe he had the happiest disposition any boy ever possessed. We used to watch him a good deal as he went about the campus. Why, he was as full of life as four ordinary Freshmen. It amused us to see him vaulting upon Blair Hall porch—he never went up the stone steps—or jumping out of the windows of Goodnow Hall. At first he just wrapped the whole faculty about his little finger, but

it wasn't a month until they found out that
that little twinkle in Davy's eye meant mischief. One night he climbed on the veranda
of the ladies' dormitory and threw the college
dog, tied up in a bag, into one of the bed-rooms.
Several bad cases of hysterics resulted.
After that, the faculty had it in for him, and
many a trip did the little fellow make to
Prexie's private sanctum. But he always
came out on top. Prex never had the heart
to be severe, and the day after the interview,
Davy was sure to be found bobbing about as
serenely as ever.

"But Davy's voice—I remember distinctly
the first time we ever heard it. It was his
first Friday morning at Chapel. Davy
bounded up the stairs just a moment late and
as the seats had not yet been assigned, he
stopped on the threshold and glanced about
for a place to sit down. I turned around just
in time to see his predicament and beckoned
to him. He saw me in an instant. Down the
aisle he marched and squeezed himself in
among the Seniors just as Prexie stood up to
give out the hymn. I offered him my book

but he turned on me with a smile and said, 'I know it, I guess,' and fixed his eyes on Prex. Well, I started out to sing, but before I was half through the first score I forgot that I ever knew how. The young Freshman evidently did 'know it'. Such a voice as that was a pretty scarce article on the front seats at Chapel, and it wasn't two minutes before every one else in that end of the room was silent. Others as well as myself were charmed with Davy's magnificent tenor.

"As we filed out of the chapel that morning I said to my chum, Jack Niles, 'What's the matter with that for Glee Club material?' 'What's the matter?' he repeated, 'why, man, it's a sure go!'

"To make a long story short," went on Stanley, leaning forward in his chair, "Davy was elected to membership in the club, and it was at the semi-weekly practice that I got to know him well. He was the life of the whole club and you can't imagine how much we thought of him. One in particular, a big, strapping Senior by the name of Tom, took him under his protection at once and the friendship that existed between those two was remarkable. It was simply great to see the way they acted. Once Davy happened to be late to a rehearsal. Tom got excited because he didn't know the reason why and couldn't find out; he made up for it by grinding out all the discord possible. Then the director got excited. He had just picked up a paper weight and ink bottle to settle matters with, when in came Davy, and Tom sang as if he had never heard a discord in his life. In every thing Tom behaved just so. He seemed to feel lost when he didn't have Davy."

"*A la* Damon and Pythias, don't you know," observed the Senior.

"Well, the weeks wore on and the Easter vacation brought with it the trip. It was an old story to some of us and we took it as a matter of course, but to the new members it was the greatest event of the year. Davy looked upon it as the best kind of an opportunity for a lark, and from the moment we rolled out of the Herndon depot he was half wild. Every station at which we stopped he was the first to reach the platform when the train slowed up, and the last to leave it when we were off again. I remember the afternoon just before we gave our first concert at Clinton. It had been drizzling all the morning and all of us except Davy had stayed religiously inside the car. A little wet weather, however, wasn't enough to dampen his spirits and if anything, he was livelier than ever. Tom stopped him once or twice and said anxiously: 'Go a little slow there, you young monkey,' at which Davy turned around with an injured air and looked him straight in the face; then they both laughed outright and Davy knew he had conquered.

"By noon the clouds partially rolled away. The sun came out and dried things up a bit and the afternoon was all that could be desired. We were due at Clinton at just four o'clock, and as the train had been delayed somewhat, the engineer was trying to make up for lost time. As we pulled into a small village about ten miles distant from Clinton, Davy took his customary position upon the rear platform. The place was small. Only two or three men lounged about the little station and Davy was just on the point of heeding Tom's advice to 'go slow', and stay where he was, when out of the station door rushed a young girl with such an expectant look on her face that all thoughts of Tom's advice were driven to the four winds. In her haste she dropped a small package which she carried in her arms. It fell with a splash into a little pool of water at her feet. That settled it. Davy plunged wildly into the air, and Tom looked out of the window just in time to see the pool of water do its work. In the next instant the young lady, the package, and Davy lay in a confused heap on the platform. A curly head, minus a hat, was just emerging from the mass when the train pulled away in the direction of Clinton.

"That was only the beginning of Davy's mishaps. He came along two hours later on a freight and sang with the crowd in the evening, but the trouble he got into from that time on would fill a book."

"Well, he was all right as I live," interrupted Ned, "I'd have done the same thing myself."

"With the same result probably," grinned
Lawrence from the hearth rug. Stanley smiled,
twirled the knob on his chair for a few moments,
and then continued.

"But the concerts—how we did enjoy them
and the receptions which always followed.
The brilliant footlights and the sea of faces,
the rollicking songs and the beautifully
dressed maidens who smiled at us from the
boxes; each had a fascination for us all, and
as for Davy, he seemed to be living in the
seventh heaven. His voice never failed to cap-
ture the audience from the start and many a
rosebud from daintily-gloved hands found its
way to his feet. He always acknowledged the
favor with a smiling bow which in itself
was enough to ensure an encore, and when he
came out to sing again his voice would be
sweeter than ever.

"After the first concert, Tom completely
lost his dignity and rushed headlong into the
dressing-room, tumbling everybody right and
left until he found Davy. Then he grabbed
the youngster with both hands and hugged
him vigorously. 'We made the biggest hit

to-night we've made for years,' he exclaimed,
'and you did it, Davy, you did it.'   Some one
cried 'Rah! Rah! Rah! Davy,' and we took it
up with a will and yelled until the very walls
shook.

"O, those were times, times a fellow don't
forget very soon either.   I'm not very much
of a crank, but I'd be willing to put the events
of those two weeks alongside of any thing
that's happened here in the last ten years.

"Finally the last concert came.   We had a
crowded house.   The numbers were received
with enthusiasm right along, but something
seemed to be lacking.   Even Davy was de-
pressed during the first part of the program,
but during the intermission he came around
with a poor attempt at a smile, and said: 'It's
the last time we'll all sing together, fellows,
but let's do our best anyway.   Every man of
us brace up a bit.'

"We tried to follow out the suggestion, and
the next two or three numbers were much
better, but it was not until we came to the
last thing on the program that we really
livened up.   That was our dear old 'Scarlet

and Black' and we couldn't help but do our best. Davy cried out just as we were filing to our places on the stage, 'Whoop 'er now, boys!' and we did it. The first two verses of the old piece:

'Sing to the college with banner so bright,
O sing to the Scarlet and Black,'

seemed to thrill us through and through. Tom looked at Davy standing in his place at the end of the line. It was the youngster's favorite. With his hands clasped behind his back and his eyes raised, he was pouring forth his whole soul.

"We were in the middle of the second stanza. Tom said afterwards that he had never felt so inspired in his life. With lightning-like rapidity he went over in his mind all the happy events of his college days. His first few weeks at school, his prowess on the football field, his membership in the Glee Club, and now he was a Senior—in a few short weeks it would all be over, but still to-night he could sing and his college song was his inspiration.

"Suddenly a sharp, clear sound like the

snapping of a pistol rose above our voices. Then a slight crash and silence.

"A long row of gas-jets attached to a large tin reflector extending the whole length of the stage, had swayed uneasily in the breeze from an open window all the evening long. The strain had told upon the small wire which held the jets and one end had given way. In falling it had fortunately caught upon a loose loop in one of the ropes which regulated the flies and hung suspended in the air at an angle of about thirty degrees.

"Davy had seen the accident first, and realized what might be the consequences. Quick as a flash he flew across the platform, up the ladder, and in an instant was bending above our heads. The gas-jets flickered dangerously near the dry and dusty flies and already one of them was smoking. Another moment and the house would be in flames. With one hand Davy steadied himself. With the other he reached out after the rope. We held our breath. He might not reach it. We saw him bend lower and in an instant the rope was in his hand, the gas-jets once more in place.

" 'Rah! Rah! Davy,' some one yelled; but the cry was never finished.

"Whether it was from dizziness or a misstep we never knew. Davy swayed and fell. Tom uttered an exclamation of horror and sprang forward with outstretched arms. It was too late. A dark heap lay there before us on the floor. We gathered around with blanched faces, as Tom sank upon his knees and took the little fellow in his great strong arms.

" 'Are you hurt? Are you hurt, Davy?' he asked hoarsely.

"For one moment the lad opened his eyes and fixed them steadily upon Tom.

" 'Tom,' he gasped, 'Tom, it's all right— tell them to go on— The Scarlet and Black—I want them—to.' And then with voices that trembled with emotion, we finished our Alma Mater's song."

There was a loud stamping of feet on the stairway and a strain of rollicking laughter came up the corridor of the Old Hall as Stanley paused. The Alpha Nu's had returned from the reception. Finally he said slowly:

"There's not much of anything left to tell.

Of course the curtain was rung down and the
audience dismissed as soon as possible. Two or
three physicians came on the stage and did
what they could, and all of us lent a hand to
make Davy comfortable. Tom had placed his
burden upon a couch in one of the dressing-
rooms but he still held the curly head in both
his hands. A consultation was hastily held.
He had suffered internal injuries, they said;
he might live a month—possibly more—but he
would never walk again. At first Tom listened as though dazed. Then he realized
what it all meant and buried his head in
Davy's curls and cried like a child."

.   .   .   .

The fire in George Lawrence's room had almost gone out when the two visitors rose to go.

"I see I've missed my train," said Stanley
drawing on his gloves, "but this is the first
time I've told that story for years, and when I
got started I couldn't stop."

"Glad you didn't," blurted out Ned as he
reached for his hat. Lawrence leaned against
the mantel-piece, seemingly absorbed in

thought.   Finally he looked up and asked
with an attempt at carelessness:

"By the way, what became of Tom?"

The visitor hesitated a moment.   "He has
been a real estate agent in one of our western
towns for the last ten years," he said, "and
people say he is doing well.   To the business world he is known as Thomas Stanley."

The Work of the Storm.

CHARLIE HILLMAN was striding at a rapid rate down the railroad, with his head hung low and his hands thrust deep into his pockets. He had the blues. When Charlie Hillman had the blues he usually felt desperate. He ought to be at the editors' meeting at the college, but then, he knew that he would only make trouble, and what did he care how the paper came out? He would graduate next week and what was the use of wasting more time? Had he not done his share already?

The day was sultry and close, and the half-haze seemed to increase the intense heat. The sun appeared like an immense ball of fire, grudgingly going on its course. A hot day is still hotter along a railroad. The sand gleams and the rails glisten with more heat than brightness. The pebbles crunched under Hillman's feet, the wires buzzed, the smothered breath

of the south wind burned his cheek; but on he
went. Where was he going? "To destruction," he might have said," and the sooner the
better." In the turmoil of his brain, he
almost wished that a train might steal upon
him and end his miserable existence. What
had he to live for? Why was he going to college? What would he do with himself next
year? He didn't care, nor did anyone. That
was just it—no one cared whether he would ever
amount to anything. No one ever sympathiz-
ed with him in his troubles. Well, there was
Maud Garland, but he had no reason to think
that she cared what he did. She would probably think him a fool if she saw him walking
off in this absurd manner. And he didn't
care what she thought. Why did she say that
he did not get his lessons as well as he should;
that he ought to like Professor Small? Why
did she ask him if he wasn't wasting his time
reading instead of studying?

With such thoughts, he plunged down the
steep embankment without noticing the blue
eyes of the late violet, peeping at him as if in
surprise at his ruthless footsteps, or the white

anemone which he loved so much at other times. He leaped over the fence as though a fiend were in pursuit. He did not stop until he came to a stream rippling gently before him. He could not jump across it. He would not turn back, so, flinging himself down, he bathed his burning face. It was a beautiful spot. The dogwoods and elders were in full blossom, and below them the purple phlox and may-apple. The enterprising buttercup at his feet was just sending out runners to start new colonies. The sedges at his side bent gracefully over the whispering ripples. Gnats and bees hummed about him. The merry note of the brown thrush, the clear-toned call of the robin might have roused him. But no; he looked on all this joyous life and beauty as only a taunt to his feelings. Why should all nature be contented and happy, and he perfectly wretched, with nothing to live for? Why was he made with a soul that must have an object in life? What was he made for, anyway?

Hours passed without his notice. The sun was sinking. He sprang to his feet and scrambled to the track with a vague sense of

his distance from home and of anxiety for his
sister, left alone. How strange the sky appeared. The sun was now gone, but the whole
western heavens glowed with brilliant red.
The soft, fleecy clouds grew black and furious, sending down long blunt fingers as
though eager to grasp the earth. A peculiar feeling of dread aroused him and with increasing
sense of concern, he hurried homeward. The
clouds piled up behind him. Before he reached
home, the lightning became fearful and the
thunder terrific. Fearing that his sister might
be frightened, he burst open the door of their
college home, and cried out:

"Lucy, where are you?"

"Here, Charlie, where have you been? Just
see what a storm is coming. You might
have been caught."

Charlie was relieved to find his sister, who
was standing in the west door, watching the
rolling, turning and twisting of the great
masses of clouds. She was not frightened
herself and even his absence did not cause her
alarm, she was so interested in the sight before her. Slowly the clouds were wound, as

about a great distaff, into one immense roll.
A shuddering stillness came upon all about
them.   Lucy unconsciously clutched Charlie's
shoulder.   A moment of breathless silence,
and then a distant roar as of a thousand cars,
which grew louder and louder; then a crash as
though heaven and earth had collided.

"Oh, Charlie, the college!" exclaimed Lucy,
and they watched the west building totter,
tremble, and fall, not as a mass, but as though
each brick were separated from the others.   It
seemed to fall almost slowly and not as the
roof and corners of Center College, which, with
a sudden lurch, took a flying leap over miles of
space.   It seemed hours as the two stood and
watched that terrible sight, yet it was scarcely
a moment between the first crash and the sudden jerk of their own house which made
Charlie catch his sister and run to the cellar.
There they crouched in fear and awe.   The
deep roar of the storm and the crash of the
trees,   the   thud   of   immense   weights,
finally gave place to the rush of roaring rain.
Down it came in torrents as though the clouds,
having failed to wreak full vengeance by wind,

had burst in their rage and poured out stream after stream of renewed wrath.

Charlie and Lucy crept upstairs, unwilling to remain longer in the dark and gloomy cellar. What a sight was revealed to them by the intermittent flashes of lightning! It was perfect chaos.

"Lucy, you are all right, I'm going to the college to help. I know there were boys in Stewart Hall, and society had begun in Center College. Hope they're not all killed." Charlie hurried from the house, but found his way obstructed. Trees, mixed with lumber in a confused mass, were piled in heaps before him; bodies of dead animals lay in his path; rushing streams of water took him off his feet. Scrambling up, he anxiously worked his way on. At last he succeeded in reaching the railroad, along which he had walked so dejectedly but a short time before. He heard sounds which made him think the evening freight had been overturned by the storm, but he could not linger for anything; he must get to the boys. By the aid of his lantern he picked his way across the campus. He surely heard voices. All were not killed, then, or perhaps others had succeeded in getting there before him.

"Here's Charlie Hillman," some one called from a group gathered by the mound of bricks, timbers, window-sashes and other wreckage of the large building, all looking as though it had been through the first grind of an immense millstone.

"Yes, I'm here. Are you all safe? Are there any in the ruins?"

"Don't know. Where's Harry?"

"Here," came a weak voice from the dark heap. A terrified look came over the boys' faces.

"Come, let's get him," and Charlie plunged forward into the mass. "Where are you, Harry?"

They suddenly came upon a form, scarcely visible by the light of the one lantern, and covered by timbers and plaster. George Trenton! How terrible! Was he dead?

"I'll run for help and give the alarm," called one as he sped away toward town. Many from near by began to come in, some with axes and saws, others with lanterns and crowbars.

No one worked with more strength and skill than Charlie Hillman. The violence of his feeling in the afternoon was only directed into another channel. Even the terrible sights about him did not chase away his rebellious thoughts. Why wasn't he under those bricks? Why was he alive and George Trenton dead, George, who had such a bright life before him? With these thoughts raging through his brain, he pulled timber from timber, sawed and pounded to release Harry Turner. A groan came to the ears of those at work. Turning, they saw George raise his head and look with dazed eyes at the sight about him.

"George, are you alive? Thank God! George is alive! I'll take care of him; you keep on with Harry."

"Boys," and there was a silence as Professor Hall spoke, "I think we can work better if we know just how many are missing. I will call the roll, and if you know where any of the others are, answer." With a quaver in his voice, the dear old Professor commenced

with the A's. "Julia Anderson." "At home,
safe," answered her brother Tom. "Then you
are here, Tom," and two were marked present.
The Professor went on checking those present
and those reported safe, but when he came to
Arthur Camden's name there was a silence that
meant more than words. He was one of the noblest of the students. There could not be a
more intense feeling of agitation and suspense
in a body of students than during those few
moments. Each feared to hear the next name
called and silently rejoiced when the answer
came, "safe". Five were not accounted
for. With sinking hearts, they turned
again to seek among the ruins for the missing
ones.

The attention of all was centered on this
one ruin, for the students from Center College
were safe except one, and it was known that
he was not in the building. A search party
had gone for him, while the rest worked to release Harry.

Suddenly a cry, "Look at Center College,"
burst from many lips. Fire! How the flames
blazed and flared! Phosphorus in the cellar!

Horrible! The books were in that building. They must be saved. Run for buckets! Call the engine! Carry the books away! Hurry with the water! What destruction— fire added to wind and rain! Such a night would never be spent on that campus again.

Charlie Hillman was again the leader. With renewed fierceness, he swung buckets from right to left. Minutes passed like hours. Exciting danger kept him absorbed for a time, but he became restless, standing in the long line. He called another to his place and went to the pump. The man at the pump was glad to be relieved. Charlie worked with untiring strength. Many wondered afterward at his remarkable endurance. The water seemed to increase the flames instead of quenching them. Their efforts would be in vain if the engine did not arrive soon. It seemed that it would never come, but if they could have seen the men with the engine, as they worked their way through the mass of ruins in the flooded streets, they would not have complained. Mud, water, fallen trees, roofs of houses, everything hindered their coming.

At last they arrived, but it was almost too late. The streams from the engine could not put out the fire, but only check its progress into the library.

Daylight. What a sight for the rising sun! The college in ruins! Hundreds of people homeless; scores of pitiful dead faces!

Morning! What would it bring? Charlie Hillman dared not think. He was glad he could spend the day working as he had spent the night. "Maud Garland!" The thought of her came over him like a flash. Was she safe, or was she in the ruins? Calling another to his work, he escaped from the crowd. He made his way through the rubbish towards the east. He had been told that the storm was less severe in that part of the town, and until now he had not feared for her safety.

He saw many working at their homes, or where their homes had been, bringing together material to protect the children, many of whom were stripped of clothing and sat shivering, huddled in groups, waiting for shelter. There was a group weeping over a dead mother. Charlie's heart recoiled in fear. Could it be that Maud was dead? Why had he not looked for her before. What an agony of suspense! He hurried on, unconscious of everything but the possibility that Maud might be dead, when he stumbled and fell beside a body stretched upon the wet ground. It was a child. With difficulty Charlie recognized Donald, Maud's little brother, whom the wind had carried several hundred feet. Poor little boy! How white his face was and what feeble breath came from his lips! Charlie wrapped his coat about him and lifted him tenderly in his arms, carrying him towards the place where his home had been.

There were a number of people gathered around the ruins of Mr. Garland's home. Charlie carried his burden to the child's father. "Mr. Garland, here is Donald. I found him but a short distance away."

"Charlie Hillman, did you come from the skies? My little Donald! Praise God! I have been working all night to find him and Maud. O my dear boy!" With manly tears, Mr. Garland took his still unconscious son and caressed him.

"I will take him to Mrs. Holland's. They have one room left which can be used for the wounded. Oh, if we could only find Maud! Can she be under the house, or was she blown away like Donald?" Charlie's heart thrilled at the word 'we'. The father had unconsciously shown him that he was a partner in anxiety for Maud.

"Where was Maud when the storm struck?" he asked.

"With Donald, in the dining-room. You see the back wall is standing, but the roof has fallen down and leans against it. She may be under that end. I have been removing everything I could, but have not heard a sound. Hark, what is that?" Charlie bounded to the spot.

"Father," and a voice in pain came from beneath the great sideboard.

"Maud!" Charlie called before the father could command his feelings.

"Mr. Garland, you take Donald and I will work here." With a muttered prayer of thanksgiving, Mr. Garland turned away. Charlie worked now with a renewed strength.

Not a forced, fierce strength, but strength brought by the love in his own heart and the encouragement Maud gave him from time to time. Somehow as he worked, she seemed to reveal to him a future for himself, and every trace of yesterday's pain and desperation vanished. Life opened with new meaning before him. Whether Maud might live, or living, love him, did not trouble him at the moment; he loved her, and that was enough. For an hour they worked, until they had moved away the great sideboard. Maud lived, and in some way he understood that she cared. Tenderly they laid her on a pile of clothing they had gathered. She lay still and helpless. Her father remained with her while Charlie went in search of a stretcher.

There was no dejection in the face of Mr. Garland as he looked upon his home in the dim, morning light. Home and everything might be taken if only Maud and Donald were spared. What were houses and lands to the loving presence of the daughter who had so well filled the place left vacant in his home. Mother and wife were gone, but the third angel which blesses a man's life, the daughter, was still with him. Life meant much to him when those trusting eyes looked into his.

Such thoughts as these filled his mind as he talked with Maud. He told her how he had hunted for her and Donald; how Charlie had found Donald, who was safe and out of danger. She forgot her pain in her joy at hearing that Donald was alive.

Upon the improvised stretcher which Charlie brought, they slowly carried her to the schoolhouse, which was turned into a hospital. A number of injured were there before them, and all the skill and tenderness possible were used to relieve them. Maud waited her turn, holding her father's hand to help bear the pain.

Charlie helped the busy men and women arrange beds, remove seats, and care for the injured. He worked in this way until the surgeon attended Maud and pronounced her injuries less serious than they had dared to hope. He cheered her with hopeful words, now that the uncertainty was over. Then he grasped Mr. Garland's hand warmly and passed silently from the room.

It was almost a feeling of exultation which filled him as he walked down the street. He left the sorrow and suffering to look again upon nature. The contrast between the devastated city and the quiet of the meadows and trees outside, was like the change in his own being; from strife and turmoil to peace and happiness. He strolled through a pasture and came to a large pond. This pond was always well known for its beautiful water-lilies. Charlie remembered Maud's fondness for the pure white flowers. He waded to some of the freshest and broke their stems. As he looked upon their delicate whiteness, he compared them to Maud. He felt the sweetness of her life appeal to him just as the perfume of the lilies appealed to his senses, stirring within him a love for the pure and true.

.   .   .   .

Home again! He stepped into the kitchen, where Lucy was preparing breakfast.

"Oh, Charlie, have you been working all night? If I hadn't been so busy I would have worried about you. Now, you must want something to eat. I'll make you some coffee in just a moment. You surely want some. Won't you rest now?"

"No, Lucy, I shall find plenty to do. What have you been doing?"

"Helping as much as I could. Did you know they are taking all the injured people to the school-house? You did? Well, I'm going to help nurse. They have asked the college girls to come. I can do as much good that way as any."

Charlie thought of Maud. "Maud is down there. She is very badly injured."

"Maud! Oh, Charlie, how is she hurt? Is it serious?"

"Not so badly as we feared. Her limbs were badly crushed and she suffers much pain, but she will live. You should have seen her when her father and I carried her down to the school-house; she was so patient. She seemed to think more about Donald than of her own suffering. I don't see how anyone can be so patient, but then Maud is always so."

"Yes, the dear girl! Can't I go down right now and see her?"

"No, let's finish our breakfast and we will

both go. I went to Malcomb's pond and got these lilies for her. Come, Lucy, don't be so grieved, we ought to be glad that it is no worse. Just think how many were killed."

"I know, it's terrible; I can hardly believe it! Poor Maud." They ate very little breakfast. In a few minutes the brother and sister were walking toward town. So intent were they upon their own thoughts that scarcely a word passed. Lucy was filled with dismay at the terrible ruin about her. It was a miracle that anyone was alive after such a storm. With a feeling of relief, they passed the ruins and came to the open streets again.

"There is Captain Douglass in his uniform. Wonder why that is? Good-morning, Captain, isn't this terrible?"

"Good-morning," said the Captain with a bow. "You are just the one I want to see. You take this list of the company in the south part of town; I will go on here, and notify the members of a call to the armory at nine o'clock. Explain in a very few words that it will be necessary to stand guard to-day over the scattered possessions of our citizens. Train-loads of people are coming in to see the sights and there may be thieving." With another bow the Captain went on. Lucy secretly wondered if anything in the world would ever stir Mr. Douglass enough to make him show any feeling.

Soon they reached the school-house. Lucy turned in. "Aren't you coming in, Charlie?"

"No. I will go to the armory. You can give these to Maud," he said, handing her the bunch of lilies.

A strange world this is. Each one so wrapped in himself, yet finding pleasure in doing some little kindness for another. Life goes in a circle; from self to others, from others to self. What is the right feeling after all?

Charlie walked along thinking these things. He hoped that Maud would find pleasure in the lilies, and that they would turn her thoughts to him. Must self be first? How otherwise? But it was only a moment that he felt so; no, life was to be lived for others—for Maud.

. . . .

It was noon. The sun was glaring down

upon the piles of ruins, and upon the distressed people who were collecting their furniture or keepsakes to begin again a home for themselves. It was the Sabbath, but the people of the town felt that they could worship God better that day by helping their neighbors than by holding church service.

Charlie Hillman stood above the immense pile of débris, gun in hand, to protect the people in their search. His grief for the homeless only increased his anger at the crowd which surged around, picking up little articles as curiosities; making rude remarks about the appearance of the people; jesting at the loss and destruction, with utter disregard for the feelings and sufferings of those about. Could people be so thoughtless as to look upon suffering as a joke? How could men, with indifference, watch a mother gather little keepsakes of her dead child? How harsh that careless laugh sounded upon the air so fraught with pain and trouble. Was all kindness of heart lost? A group of young men, insolently puffed their cigars and turned away with a joke, when asked by two young boys to help remove a heavy timber from a slightly damaged piano. That was a little thing, but typical of the crowd. Hundreds came and looked upon the distress as upon a circus, with a prying curiosity which was cruel to the sufferers.

Charlie watched all this, and anger and shame blazed on his cheek. It was a new view of humanity. Was this the world in which he was to try life? Would all be as selfish as these? No; and then he thought of Maud. He did not care what others were; he would live for her. He rejoiced that there was something above all this sordidness. So the day went on, distress and disregard before his eyes, but kindness in his heart. Charlie could scarcely realize that it was only yesterday that he walked down the railroad track in such a reckless mood. When he was relieved of guard duty, he felt as though he had been living in such scenes for an age. At last, he felt the need of rest for mind and body. He would see Maud, and then he could pass the night in sleep.

It was a sad yet pretty sight which met his

eyes when he entered the hospital. White curtains and drapings, with here and there bouquets of June flowers, made the place seem pure and sweet. There was much suffering, but more patience; and there were some smiles for him as he passed down the room. Maud welcomed him, and thanked him for the lilies. He watched her with loving glance as she fondled her little brother sitting with his head near her own. Her gentle love and patience made him almost reverence her. He no longer wished he was under that pile of bricks, and he felt that he had as bright a life before him as George Trenton. Life meant more to him now, although a cyclone from heaven was needed to bring the revelation.

The Professor's Story.

IT WAS the last evening in December, and it seemed as if the skies themselves were draped in sorrow for the dying year. The smoke hung low in the streets, and mingling with the slowly drifting mist, veiled the college town of Herndon in a mantle of gloom.

Professor Townsend's residence on Campus Square loomed in the struggling light of the street lamps, frowning and stern as a prison. Yet once within and all was changed. The large parlors, still adorned with Christmas holly and other bits of winter greenery, were filled with guests. A fire that would have added cheer to any yule-tide blazed brightly in a wide hearth. Its dancing beams imparted a pleasing warmth to the old paintings and adorned with curious reflections a profusion of vases, statuettes, bric-a-brac and other treasured mementos of the host's journeyings far afield.

It was a watch-night function, and as Professor Townsend's capabilities as a host were in high repute on Campus Square, the faculty was out in force. The mourning skies, with their trailing shrouds of fog and smoke had not stained a single face with sadness. Glad welcome for the new year that would be born with the morning rang in every voice. It shone in the beaming faces of staid matrons, and again in the unwonted vivacity of the demure lady teachers from the academy. It was reflected anew in the unrestrained good humor of the senior professors, and was focussed almost to ignition in the animation of the younger instructors. This glow of good nature melted scholastic reserve and class-room seriousness, and soon reduced even the most refractory elements to a delightful fusion.

The gifted host scientifically placed every guest in contact with the proper opposite, so that not a single discordant note marred the social harmony. He paired the austere senior professor with Miss Lamar, the instructress in French. Her vivacity and wit were contagious and soon his wintry face beamed like a June morning. The diffident young geologist was entrusted to the lady principal, a genial soul whose mere presence was a benediction to a bashful man. The youthful but eccentric Professor Rolleston was consigned to the social mercies of the amiable hostess. Every guest was made at ease and soon the rooms were filled with the confused hum of voices. The stream of merry sound flowed on, broken continually by ripples of laughter, and lashed now and then almost to undergraduate boisterousness by the jokes of the facetious Latin professor.

Music came and then refreshments, after which the host rose and said: "We will consider the long couch at the angle of the fire-place a sort of prisoners' bench. The bachelors of this company will seat themselves thereon and await sentence." After arranging the remainder of the company in a wide semi-circle facing the smiling culprits and turning off the lights so that only the beams from the hearth lighted the expectant faces, he continued, with feigned seriousness:

"The bachelor is multiplying among us and in connection therewith I have noted another significant fact. The genus *Spinster* which was once an exotic and rarely bloomed among us, now appears quite naturalized in our midst. Our bachelors are certainly reprehensible, and I take it, that any civilized method of domestication will meet with approval. Bachelors, stand up, while I pronounce doom! In partial expiation, you shall each relate, for the edification of this watch-night gathering, some interesting experience of your college life. Total expiation will doubtless prevent a repetition of this sentence, for the new year is a multiple of four. Professor Carter is first on my card."

The junior members, as a body, were men of unusual talents, and some rare tales followed. Several were fresh from foreign scenes and two had penetrated the mystic veil of the orient. Some narrated with delightful informality; others, for contrast, embellished their tales with many elegancies of the story-telling art. Even the timid geologist surprised the company with a capital story of Oberlin days. To

the pleased listeners each new tale seemed more
captivating than the last.   The penalty in-
flicted apparently in jest resulted in a royal
contest.

The group of the condemned thinned, one
by one, until only Professor Rolleston remained.   Then the interest slackened, for the
company felt that the story-telling was at an
end. No one had ever known Professor Rolleston to lay aside his peculiar reserve, during
his two years in the chair of history.   The
opinion prevailed that, whatever his ability in
the class-room, outside of it he was decidedly
an enigma, and that socially, at least, he was
an insignificant figure.   The instructress in
French shrugged her shoulders, and leaning
toward her companion, confided in a low tone:
"I am sure Professor Townsend has made a
mistake this time. The idea of saving Professor Rolleston until the last! Why, any one
of them, even our shy geologist, would have
done better! It's a pity to spoil such a program with an anticlimax."

Professor Rolleston rose.   There was a re-
fined strength in his clean-cut features, but

his dark, far-gazing eyes gave an expression of almost mysterious reserve and abstraction to his sober face. He began by explaining, in a hesitating, embarrassed manner, that the host had asked him the day before to be ready with some story of his student days.

"Professor Townsend knew," he went on, "that I spent part of my college life on the Pacific Coast, and suggested that I relate some incident of my life there. I had my share of adventures, but I could not entertain you by trying to tell them. I am not a story-teller, so I asked if I might read one instead. During my senior year at Berksly, I had an unusual experience on New Year's eve. I spent the vacation in the Sonoma country looking up material in old Spanish records, for an historical essay. Late in the afternoon of the last day of the year, I set out upon a drive of twenty miles to the little seaside village of Villanne. The road was unexpectedly difficult, the fog came in and I got lost in the coast hills. I finally found shelter at a ranch-house. What my hostess told me that night impressed me so deeply that I wrote it out the

next day while her words were fresh in
memory. It is a sober story, but I thought it
might not be out of place to read it to you in
this last hour of the departing year."

His hesitation was disappearing now and all
eyes were turned upon his grave, earnest face.
Yet the attention was prompted more by curiosity than by any anticipation of what was to
follow. The hostess placed a reading lamp so
that its screened beams fell upon his man-
uscript. The touch of the pages was an inspiration, an open sesame to a new side of his
nature. He seemed to change before them
and the unexpected revelation gave his words
peculiar charm and power. In a voice which
gathered earnestness and pathos as he went
on, he read the following story:

After wandering about in ink-like darkness, it
seemed for hours, completely confused and bewildered, there suddenly appeared a glow in
the fog. My horse stopped short and would
not budge. Then it flashed upon me that
perhaps I had reached the brink of some

precipice near the ocean, and that the glow
came from a signal light upon an opposing
cliff. Somewhat frightened, I groped my way
cautiously around to my horse's head. But,
instead of finding the edge of an abyss, I
struck my head solidly against a beam, and,
for a moment, the whole firmament blazed
with signals. Yet I never received a more
welcome jolt. The beam was a part of a
huge gate with a roadway leading through it.
I opened it and leading my exhausted horse
slowly up the lane, found a large ranch-house,
from a window of which the light was stream-
ing into the fog. I went to the door and
knocked. It was promptly opened, and in
the light that flooded through it, stood a gray-
haired woman with large, black, flashing eyes,
who surveyed me keenly from head to foot.

"Well, sir, what do you want here?" was
the abrupt greeting which followed her searching glance. For an instant I was confused.
She had not given me time to say, 'Good evening.' Then, realizing the seriousness of my
plight, I said: "I want a place to stay over
night, some supper for myself and shelter for

my horse. I started from Santa Rosa for Villanne about sunset. I have lost my way in the fog, and my horse is tired out."

"Well, you haven't travelled very fast then. You are some distance off the direct road, but all you have to do is to keep on down the coast for seven miles. I don't like to keep strangers," she replied curtly.

I answered with some earnestness: "My horse cannot stand it. Even if I shouldn't get lost again, he will never pull me through seven miles of stones and sand to-night. If you can't keep me, I shall have to sleep out in the fog." She did not reply for an instant. Then suddenly her whole manner changed, and, in a softened, almost tremulous voice she said: "I can't let you do that. My accommodations are not just what I should like to offer, but you are welcome. Come in and dry yourself. My man will attend to your horse and I will get you something to eat."

I thanked her warmly, and, entering, found myself in a large living room, with a deep recess or kitchen at one side. There was a cheerful fire, and by a window, there was a table with a number of books and the lamp that had lighted me in through the fog. The furniture, though old-fashioned, betokened a fairly prosperous owner, and there was such an appearance of order and comfort that I began to feel at home at once.

My hostess called the ranchman and soon had my supper steaming over the fire. Her manner was kindness itself and there was an air of intelligence and refinement about her, that aroused my interest deeply. As I sat, warming my benumbed hands and stretching my stiffened limbs, I began to speculate upon her position and history. The wrinkles of her pale face seemed deeply written records of struggle and sorrow. Yet there was strength and determination also. Her positive manner, the promptness and authority with which she gave her orders to the ranchman, together with the minute directions which she added to her commands, proved that she was master there and the only one. Yet why should such a woman live alone in this wilderness? And again, what had so suddenly altered her manner towards me?

But at this point my speculations were interrupted by her call to supper. She seated herself opposite me and waited upon me attentively. After a few questions concerning my journey, she suddenly asked: "You are from the East, are you not? You haven't been long on the coast."

Somewhat surprised, I answered: "Yes, I am from the East. My parents are New Yorkers. I have been in the West two years." She said, "I was sure that you were a newcomer. There is a certain air and accent about people from the far East. I recognize an Easterner almost at first sight." Then after a slight pause she added. "Still it isn't many that I see in this wilderness."

There was a tone of sadness in this last remark that started anew my train of speculations. We talked on in commonplaces until I finished my meal. Detecting occasionally what I judged an anxious look, I determined to allay if possible any suspicion or fear which she might have concerning me. So I explained, in detail, my errand to Villanne, and then related how I came to the coast to im-

prove my health, continue my studies and to
see more of the world.

"And unlike most new-comers," I went on,
"I have not been homesick for a single day.
I spend most enjoyable vacations in the moun-
tains and at the seashore, seeing more of
nature and less of men. I am getting on well
at college also. During the past two years at
Berksly ——."

But I did not finish my sentence. At the
name Berksly, she sank back in her chair with
a stifled moan, and covered her face with her
hands. In a moment she recovered herself
but there were tears in her eyes as she said in
a voice full of emotion: "Berksly, Berksly,
you do not know what sorrow that name
awakes in me. I have sometimes wished that
Berksly had been sunk in the middle of the
bay."

She paused a moment and then the tears
came like rain. I was silent. Her grief was
too deep for one who did not share it to comfort, yet she noticed my silent sympathy, and
struggling to control her emotion, went on: "I
know it is a weak and foolish thing to cry, but

there have been many times when I would have
given all that I owned for tears. Your sudden coming has moved me deeply, and I feel
that I must tell you why. Your young face
and Eastern accent have taken me back to the
time when I was young and hopeful. My
parents too, were New Yorkers, and when I
was young I had all that money and social
position could give. I attended the best
schools and took a high rank. Friends
prophesied great triumphs for me. I was
called beautiful and it must have been true,
for I know that I was proud and had would-be
lovers by the score. I was Milton Sherwood's
daughter, and would inherit not only wealth
but the prestige of an old family name.

"Among the many who crowded around me
there was one whose mere presence was a charm.
He was manly and handsome, and esteemed me
too highly to weary me with flattery. We became fast friends and in time, though I never
acknowledged it, lovers. I was proud and rich.
He was a poor young lawyer with no resources
but his education and his active brain. I
could not see how even love could bridge the

gulf between his position and mine.   One day
a decisive moment came, and though my pride
made me say, friendship, it cost me inexpressible
pain.   It seemed as if I had sacrificed my soul.

"And then in a period of benumbed relaxa-
tion I allowed a broker's son to pay me his
court.   He was a commonplace young man
but he had money and a long line of aristo-
cratic ancestors.   The social world was delighted, our parents approved, and we were
married.   But there was a hollowness in my
affection for him because there was an empti-
ness in my life when I realized that he whom my
inmost heart had worshipped had gone out of
it forever.   Yet I tried to forget, for I knew
what had been done was irrevocable. I wished
to make my husband happy.   He should not
suffer through my mistaken pride.

"A child was born, and, in addition to the
passion of motherhood, all the pent-up love
of my heart was lavished upon that boy.   I
had something to live for and a new and
stronger tie bound me to my husband.   Soon
his baby prattle and the patter of his little feet
broke the silence of our old house.   But one

summer morning as the nurse and I were starting for a drive, he slipped away from us, and
before we missed him, was in the street. The
next moment I heard a shout and saw a dray-
man, with a look of horror in his face, bring
his horses upon their haunches. But it was
too late. My child was crushed before my
eyes.

"More light went out of my life that summer
morning than I thought could ever return to
it again. My loss seemed a judgment sent
upon me for being untrue to the holiest passion I had known. Then I hated my false
pride, and the false value I had placed upon
money. In my wild grief I began to hate the
city and almost to loathe our home. The pave-
ments seemed cruel and blood-stained, and
each time a heavy load went rumbling by, that
terrible scene would flash upon me and drive
me wild.

"Just then the news of gold in California
reached New York, and a frenzy of excitement
followed. One day my husband came home
and said that a company of merchants had
chartered a ship to Aspinwall, and that if I

would consent he would sail with them for the gold fields. I answered, 'Take me with you and you can go.' He argued the dangers and hardships, but I was young and daring and the idea took hold upon me like an inspiration. Life in the city had become unbearable, and I hailed escape from it as a slave hails freedom. Danger and hardship would be welcome if they brought relief from the remorse and grief that distracted me.

"My will prevailed, and we sailed, leaving behind home, parents, friends, and all the luxuries of our wealth for an unknown future in an unknown land. The journey was long and hard, but we reached San Francisco safely, passed up to Sacramento and joined a pack-train for the foot-hills. There were many trials by the way, but the wildness and novelty of the scene, and a secret exultation at my triumph over the unusual, bore me up.

"How I survived what followed at the mines, I cannot tell. I saw continually around me, strong men die from fever, from exposure, from homesickness and despair. Many were the dying hands I held in mine, and many were the last messages I wrote to wives and sweethearts across the plains. And as I wrote those sad farewells of strong men to those for whose sake they had dared to face such dangers, my own grief lost its sharpness.

"My husband shared the common fortune of the gold hunter, sometimes rich, sometimes almost without a dollar, but always full of confidence that there was a great fortune just ahead. But, at last, after a very disastrous year, he came to me and said: 'Mary, I put all I had in the Victoria except a few hundred. It's a complete failure, and it's all gone. I'm completely discouraged. Come, let us go down to the coast and begin over again.'

"So we came here, bought a thousand acres of the Spanish owner for a trifling sum, and began sheep-raising in a modest way, for all our former wealth had been lost at the mines. Those were wild, free days, though some were long and lonesome. Traces of my old sorrow came back at times, but time and distance had removed the bitterness and the sting. I had grown into a new life in a new land.

"We prospered. I became more and more contented and into this contentment came a great joy. It was another son, the child of my maturest womanhood, strong and beautiful, and how I loved him! It was more than any girlish mother's love. It was the strong love of ripe years, made tender by trial and sorrow, and made holy by the memory of the little one snatched from me years before."

My hostess was silent for a moment. I looked up and saw that her eyes were fixed upon something far away, and for a moment her face lighted with an expression which I shall never forget as she recalled the purest passion known on earth, a mother's love for her child.

Then she continued: "The child grew and it seemed as if all I had ever dared to hope for unfolded with his unfolding life. All the grief and remorse and rebellion of my earlier life faded out in the presence of my joy. Every passion of my heart and every energy of my soul was centered upon the child. And should he know sorrow as I had known it? Never, and I banished the past.

"The years passed more quickly than the months do now, and my Harry grew to boyhood. He showed a studious turn of mind, and for his sake I became a student again. Books which I had not touched for twenty years were opened, and subjects not thought of since my seminary days were taken up anew. Before he was born all the gold in the Sierras would not have tempted me to touch any thing that would raise up the cruel ghosts of the past. Harry had an active mind and we planned to prepare him for college. I was to go with him to the city while my husband was to divide his time between the city and the ranch.

"But at this time my husband, while on his way to market was caught in a cold rain. Pneumonia resulted, and in two weeks Harry was fatherless. The poor boy seemed like one stunned, and perhaps was never quite himself again. My own grief was deep, for my husband was always kind, and in his quiet way, loved me with a constancy which none of our varied fortunes ever shook. It was not his fault that I had not been always happy, and I knew it all too well.

"All plans for Harry's schooling were broken. I dared not entrust the management of the ranch to a stranger, for it was our only source of income, and I could not bear to think of sending Harry away alone. But after two more years of study together, I felt it my duty to send him to college. So he went to Berksly. At first it was hard to stay out in these lonely hills without him, but he succeeded so well and was so hopeful and happy that I soon learned to bear it. He worked hard and earnestly and made a good record. At the end of the second year, the president wrote me that he was the strongest man in his class.

"In his junior year he was selected one of the speakers for the intercollegiate debate. He threw himself into preparation with great earnestness. He wrote that Berksly had the weaker side, that one of the speakers against them was the finest student-orator in the State, consequently it would take the hardest kind of work to win. He complained of a lack of time, and at last I consented to his remaining until after the debate before visiting home. I, too, was anxious that he should win. It would be a double reward for the years of study with him, if, besides leading his class, he should make his mark in debate.

"As the winter wore away, I noticed that his letters were peculiar, but thought it due to his great interest in the coming contest.

"At last the day came. That evening I sent my man to the telegraph station to await news. At midnight he came back with two messages that made me the proudest woman on the coast that night. One was from Harry and said: 'Mother, we have won.' The other was from the president and read: 'Berksly wins. Your son's work did it.' If I had known that his work was his life blood, and that the triumph was to be purchased at such cost!

"On the second evening afterward in just such a fog as this I heard a knock at the door. I opened it, and before it stood a college friend of Harry's. 'Harry is sick,' he said, 'and the doctors said we should take him home at once. It's nervous prostration. Overwork and too much mental strain did it, but I think home and mother will bring him out all right.' At first I was not seriously alarmed, but when they brought him in as weak as a child, and I saw his pale, changed face, the walls seemed to fall in upon me. I felt that the last blow had struck.

"A fever followed and he did not rally. Physicians from the city came, but could not help him. Yet they said when the rains stopped and spring came, there would probably be a change for the better. Spring came. The poppies and cream-cups blossomed on the hills. The warm sunshine and pure air were life-giving, but they wrought no change in Harry. He became only the shadow of my once beautiul boy. With a despairing heart I watched his departing life until one May morning it went out forever.

"I buried him beside his father and with him I seemed to bury every hope. And, oh, what months of cruel, crushing sorrow followed! In my first grief I thought I saw a hand of justice and I rebelled only against myself. But in this I rebelled against all in a bitter, despairing agony of soul. I cannot tell you how long and hard and painful the strife was, but here, all alone with the sky and the hills and the ocean, I have struggled out of that bitterness into peace—not unbroken, not perfect, but real and comforting to my sorely sorrowing heart.

"And here I am, alone and old. I attend to the affairs of my ranch and I always shall. I cannot leave it though I could well afford to live away. But my husband died here and my Harry died here and I shall stay here till the end. You are the first student who has visited here since those who came to bury their class-mate, my boy. There is something in your face which has drawn me to you and moved me to tell you my story. You are too young to realize it now, perhaps, yet sometime you may do well to remember it. But it is late and you are tired. I have wearied you too long with an old woman's troubles. There's a light in your room at the end of the hall." And then glancing at the clock she added: "Unless you are in a hurry, I won't call you too early in the morning."

When the professor, with flushed face,

suffused eyes and melting earnestness of voice,
finished his tale there was an almost solemn
stillness in the dimly-lighted room, and no
one wished to be the first to break it. Before
any one spoke, the chapel bell began to toll
out the last moments of the year. The circle
sat in silence till the wild clangor of bells and
shrill screaming of whistles announced the
new. The host turned on the lights; the
company arose, exchanging greetings and
good-wishes and began to gather around Professor Rolleston. The first to reach him was
the instructress in French. She grasped his
hand with a warm New Year's greeting and
with glistening eyes, she earnestly expressed
her appreciation. Then others pressed around
and fairly confused the modest professor with
praise and compliment. He was still the center of an admiring group when the guests began to depart.

At last when this group was dispersing, the
Latin professor touched the host upon the
shoulder, directed his attention to it with a
glance, smiled significantly and said: "Our
enigma has revealed himself and I am sure we

are all charmed with the revelation. Besides
he has completely captured our impulsive
Miss Lamar. His romance and pathos have
gone straight to her sympathetic heart. See!
They are still talking by the mantel. Ah!
They are going away together. Professor
Townsend, I fear this will result in total ex-
piation!"